Battling the Enemy

M.E. Clayton

ISBN: 978-1-64570-432-4

DEDICATION

For all the readers who wanted Deke's story –
I just hope I wrote it to your expectation!.

BATTLING THE ENEMY

CONTENTS

ACKNOWLEDGMENTS

First, foremost, and always, I want to thank my family for their support. They continue to support me unconditionally and they were so excited for me when I told them how these books came at the request of my readers.

Second, and always, will be Kamala. Next to my family, she is truly one of the biggest parts of this journey. I can't thank her enough for being the best beta ever!

And, of course, I want to thank everyone who took a chance on me when they bought this book! I understand the risk when you spend your money on a new name. Thank you, so much, for being a part of my experience.

BATTLING THE ENEMY

PROLOGUE

The one thing about Melissa Randall was the bitch sure did know how to suck a good cock.

The party was in full swing, with the bonfire blazing on the sand near the shoreline, and uninhibited teenage kids everywhere drinking, dancing, snorting up coke, popping back ecstasy, or flat out fucking. We were a dangerous lot, that's for sure; teenage kids with too much money and no supervision. It didn't matter that we were underage. It didn't matter that half the shit going on here could land us in jail.

We were untouchable.

The children of the One-Percent who didn't answer to anyone.

When we arrived at the party earlier, I had no intentions on hooking up with anyone. I had showed up just to drink and hang out. But Melissa had been on my shit all night and, admittedly, it's been a while since I unloaded down a girl's throat.

Hell, I haven't had any action since Roselyn put an end to our arrangement a couple of months ago. I can't say I was sad about it, though. As much as I adored Roselyn, she and Liam were made for each other. I always knew I was just extra, and I never had a problem with that.

But, never having been used to abstinence, it hadn't taken much for me to cave to Melissa's suggestions after a few beers. So, when she dragged me behind a cluster of trees for some half-ass privacy, I let her.

However, I wasn't so drunk that I hadn't put a condom on before she sunk to her knees. A lot of people might argue that it's just a blowjob, but I paid attention during sex-ed. Those pictures of mouth herpes had stuck with me. Besides, not judging or anything, but Melissa was awfully friendly with Sands Cove's male population. Plus, the condom was flavored. I was thoughtful like that.

I looked down, and I couldn't deny she was doing her part. My dick was down her throat with her hand working my balls as she moaned like a porn

1

star. I had my hands tangled in her dark red hair, and I held her firm as I fucked her mouth with my eight-inch cock. And, even with a condom on, that shit felt good.

I tightened my hands in her hair, getting ready to work up to completion, when a sound to my left caught my attention. I turned my head, and saw something-or rather, *someone* I never thought I'd ever see watching me get my dick sucked.

Now, it wasn't that I was a stranger to voyeurism. I've been to my fair share of parties that had been full of debauchery and shamelessness, but I've never been to a party where Delaney Martin was in attendance and *she* was the one being the voyeur.

Delaney Martin.

I watched as her eyes were taking in Melissa on her knees before me. I knew from where Delaney stood that she couldn't actually see my dick in Melissa's mouth, but even from a distance, I could tell the look on Delaney's face wasn't one of disgust.

She was captivated by what she was seeing and, suddenly, Melissa was no longer the person getting me off. The tingles developing at the base of my spine were because Delaney was watching. The burst of lust was so profound, my fists tangled and pulled on Melissa's red hair, and I started fucking her bruised lips as if I was inside her easy pussy. And because my eyes were still on Delaney, I didn't miss how she noticed the change. Her eyes shot up to my face and that's when I saw it.

Pure fucking *desire.*

Our eyes met, and I was certain she'd turn red with embarrassment and take off running, but she didn't. Her gaze held mine as I pumped my cock down Melissa's throat a few more times before finally throwing my head back, closing my eyes, and cumming in the girl's mouth.

When I opened my eyes, Delaney was gone.

Oh, hell fucking no.

I pulled my dick out of Melissa's mouth, pulled the condom off, tied that bitch up, and stuck it in my pocket. I'd rather have a busted used condom of my spunk in my pocket than become a Lifetime movie topic where some psychotic bitch turkey basted my sperm to trap me into marriage.

Melissa looked up at me from where she was still on her knees. "Deke?"

Now, here's the thing-I had nothing against, uh, friendly girls, I just didn't like when they tried to act like what this was isn't what it was always going to be.

I looked down at her as I stuffed my dick back in my pants. "Thanks for taking the edge off, Melissa, but I have to go," I told her. She pouted as I further explained, "I caught a deer in my crosshairs and it just ran off."

CHAPTER 1

Deke ~

I left Melissa on her knees in the trees as I ran after Delaney Martin.

I wasn't exactly sure what it was that had me chasing after her, but the second she met my stare and hadn't shied away from watching me cum, something snapped in me.

I'd been going to school with Delaney Martin all my life, and she had never made a splash on anyone's radar. It wasn't that she wasn't pretty enough or built, but I'd always taken her for an introvert. She never participated in our unsupervised antics. She never acted out of pocket. She never caused any drama. Delaney Martin was your typical wallflower. She had been all the years that I've known who she was.

But, tonight, that wallflower stood hidden behind the trees as she watched me get my dick sucked. Delaney hadn't stumbled upon me and Melissa and run away shocked at her intrusion. She hadn't turned away when she realized what was happening. And she sure as fuck hadn't run off embarrassed when she got caught.

No.

She kept watching, and the darkness in me that I worked hard to keep hidden stirred.

Delaney watched me cum, and so, it was only fair that I got to do the same thing.

As I came flying out of the thicket of trees and brush, my eyes scanned the throng of people everywhere in search of a brunette in a bright purple shirt. There was no way I was going to let Delaney Martin get away from me.

When I rushed past Ramsey, Liam, Emerson, and Roselyn, Ramsey and Liam immediately stood up when they noticed my preoccupation. I waved them down letting them know everything was fine as I passed them. That was the beauty of unconditional love and loyalty; no questions ever needed to be asked.

I finally found her on the hill near where all our cars were parked, tugging on her friend Ava's arm. But Ava had a beer in one hand, while nestled on Marcos Sergio's lap, and she didn't look like she was ready to leave. That assumption was confirmed the closer I got, and I noticed that Marcos had his hand up Ava's skirt.

Ever since I've known Ava Hill, she has always been a wild child. She was a knockout with her long blonde hair, big blue eyes, and a body that boasted of hot sex and wild fantasies. And, unfortunately for catty girls everywhere, Ava was also smart as a whip. She might look like a dumb blonde, but I'd bet money she'll be the head of her own Mob syndicate one day.

But, while Ramsey and Liam have both fucked her a time or two throughout the years, I've never gone there with her. Not because she wasn't capable of getting my dick hard, but because she was too…off for my taste. Now, I wasn't pretending to be a saint or selective, but I didn't get off on girls who were fucked in the head. I wanted easy fucks with clean breaks, and Ava always struck me as the type of girl who could turn on you in a heartbeat. But, admittedly, I didn't know her that well. I just knew what I've heard about her.

I never understood how she and Delaney had become friends. Those two seemed like night and day, but they were tight as fuck. For all of Ava's commanding ways, I'd never seen or heard of her treating Delaney badly. This wasn't a case of having an ugly friend you could bully to make yourself feel better about yourself. From what I could tell, they were genuinely good friends.

Granted, Delaney could never be cast in the role of the ugly friend because Delaney Martin was far from ugly. Her hair was a dark brunette but had different shades of that dark brown decorating the top of her 5'3" frame. She had keen brown eyes under a set of perfectly arched brows. Delaney could be described as pixie-like with her pert nose and high cheeks, but she had a set of lips on her that were made for sucking some lucky guy's cock.

The girls' Windsor Academy uniforms had a choice of slacks or skirts, and while most of the girls chose to wear the skirt, I'd never seen Delaney in anything other than the standard Windsor top and pants. It was like she purposely tried to hide her figure, but it was no use. Delaney Martin had a woman's body made up of a healthy-sized rack and wide hips.

But the best thing about her?

Delaney had this scar that started on the apple of her right cheek and slashed back towards her ear. It looked as if her face had gotten caught on a wire or something and had ripped her face open.

Ramsey had a scar that ran from his right eyebrow across his eye and stopped at the edge of his nose, but it was a clean scar. It was a straight line. He had gotten it when we were 8-years-old and his father had wanted to teach him a lesson in control. Little did his father know what kind of psychopath he was grooming Ramsey to become one day.

But here's the thing that had always fascinated me about Delaney's scar, her parents were just as filthy rich as the rest of the families in Sands Cove, but she never got plastic surgery to remove the scar.

She wore it proudly, never shielding it with her hair or applying layers and layers of makeup to make it less visible. Nope. Delaney had a jagged scar that tore across the side of her face and I found an immense amount of strength in that.

Delaney Martin might be a wallflower, but she wasn't weak.

Just…different.

I saw Ava's eyes widen as she saw me approach, and Marcos head nodded me, but I ignored everyone around me as I grabbed Delaney by her arm and yanked her towards me. She looked up at me and her big brown eyes widened, and if I didn't know better, I'd say she was holding her breath.

Fuck, she was pretty.

Low enough for her ears only, I whispered, "Did you like what you saw, Delaney?" This time her face did redden with embarrassment. "What part did you like best? Did you like seeing Melissa sucking my dick or were you wishing you had been Melissa?"

Delaney's eyes narrowed and I could see the tick in her jaw from trying to exercise some restraint. The last thing she wanted was for everyone around us to find out she'd been watching me get a blowjob. It didn't go with her good girl persona. "Let me go," she whispered harshly.

Even though I was ignoring everyone else around us, I was very aware that everyone had stopped whatever bullshit they had been up to, and were now focused on the two of us. I've never run after a chic before and the fact that I had now was bound to catch people's attention. "Not until I get my answer," I told her brining my other hand up to clasp her other arm, showing her I was serious.

I had Delaney in my grip, her body backed up against someone's car, while my body blocked her from the party's view, and you know what? My dick started getting hard even though I had just shot my load only a few moments earlier.

Staring down at Delaney, I would never have guessed this girl would be the girl that would change everything. Things were changing, and I knew they were changing because it wasn't the feel of her body up against mine that was making me hard. It wasn't my bruising hold on her arms that had me rock hard.

Nope.

It was that motherfucking scar on her face that kept drawing my attention.

My eyes kept flicking towards it and I could feel this quiet hum in my blood warning me of danger. I was so focused on that crude marking on her face, I hadn't heard anyone approach. It wasn't until I heard Ramsey's voice did reality finally breach the trance she had me under. "Deke, everything cool?" he asked.

No.

No, everything wasn't cool. Quiet, invisible, solitary Delaney Martin was fucking me up, and I hadn't even had enough beers to blame it on the alcohol.

My mind couldn't rid itself of the image of Delaney burrowed behind the trees watching me; watching Melissa get me off. And I couldn't ignore that it was my connection to Delaney, in that moment, that had made me shoot off like a rocket in Melissa's mouth. Melissa had become a nonfactor the second my eyes landed on Delaney.

My words were for Ramsey, but everyone invested in our little scene could hear me. "Everything's perfect, Ram," I assured him. "Me and Delaney are just having ourselves a conversation, is all."

Because Ramsey and Liam knew me so well, I heard Liam snort behind me, and Ramsey let out a deep sigh. Again-no questions asked. Ramsey and Liam were already on board with whatever I was doing without even asking what it was I was doing. Ramsey just asked if I was cool because that's all he cared about. He didn't care *what* I was doing; he just cared that I was okay while doing it, and Liam was pretty much of the same mind.

Emerson and Roselyn wisely kept quiet because, while we might all be friends, those girls knew better than to push past where they belonged. I loved them both to pieces, but Emerson's control didn't extend beyond Ramsey and Roselyn's control, no matter how close we were, didn't extend beyond Liam.

But what they did do?

They joined Ramsey and Liam in standing at my back so that Delaney and I were closed off from prying eyes as much as possible. However, turns out I hadn't needed to worry about shielding Delaney from the crowd.

Her quiet, demur, wallflower persona was shed the second she pushed at my chest and yelled, "No, we're not, Deke. Now get the hell off me!"

CHAPTER 2

Delaney ~

I was embarrassed-no, *humiliated.*

I had never even wanted to come to this stupid party. I didn't go to teenage parties, because that wasn't me.

Ava guilt tripped me with ramblings of this being our senior year and our times together were coming to an end, yadda, yadda, yadda. And so, I caved because for all of Ava's wild ways, she's been my best, and often, only friend for years.

It wasn't that I had anything against normal teenage life, but nothing about the kids from Sands Cove was normal, and that included me.

My life was already carved out for me, so I didn't see the point in dating or partying. I was destined to be a socialite wife whose job would be to help make her husband flourish. I was to be the arm candy that, that in itself was a joke, because I wasn't even that pretty. I had brown hair, brown eyes, and my body could do with a bit of dieting. But that didn't matter; my parents had already set my life on a particular path, and that was that.

The only reason I worked my ass off in school was because, even if I was destined to just be someone's wife, I didn't want to be a stupid one. I wanted to be able to talk finance, politics, etc. I didn't want to spend the rest of my life discussing the latest nail trends or shoe collection.

So, I spent my teenage years in the library or classroom instead of at parties or with a boyfriend. I was a virgin with an uncomplicated life. Or it had been before Deke Marlow caught me watching him getting a blowjob from Melissa Randall.

As soon as we had arrived, Ava immediately had a beer in her hand and powder on the tip of her nose. I never judged her for being wild because she's never judged me for being a weird nerd, but her partying always worried me a bit. But it wasn't until she landed on Marcos Sergio's lap that I knew I needed to make myself scarce. While I've gotten used to Ava's drugs and alcohol party ways, I wasn't too keen on watching Marcos finger fuck her in front of everyone. I had taken a stroll to avoid the sexual scenes often played out at these parties only to catch Deke Marlow getting his dick sucked.

Oh, the irony.

I hadn't meant to watch, either. That's the bad thing about all this. Never having been to one of these parties before, I had gotten lost in the thicket of trees. When I heard some noises, I had really believed I had found someone to save me.

Nope.

That wasn't the case at all.

When I had peeked around that cursed oak tree, my feet had frozen at the sight of Melissa Randall on her knees in front of Deke Marlow. Now, while I was a virgin, I wasn't a sheltered one. I knew exactly what was going on, and curiosity had gotten the better of me. I've never given a blowjob before, and I was enthralled at what Melissa was doing. I was pathetically taking pointers.

It wasn't until I saw Deke's hands tighten in her hair that I felt a sudden pulse between my legs. He had been anchoring himself as he began really driving into her mouth. My eyes had shot up and when they met Deke's eerie green gaze, sparks of heat curled deep in the pit of my stomach and I knew I was in trouble. And, Sweet Baby Jesus, when he kept looking at me as he fucked Melissa mouth, I knew in that moment what it felt like to be turned on.

His question pissed me off because his snide accusation had been spot on. For a split second I had wished I were Melissa on my knees before Deke. I wanted to be the one to feel those rough hands tighten in my hair. So, when he finally closed his eyes and threw his head back as he came, I ran.

I fucking *ran.*

I ran so blindly, I miraculously found myself back at the party. I saw Ava, and I hadn't cared that she was drunk, high or getting fingered in front of everyone. I wanted to leave before Deke came out of the trees, because once the lust had died down, I had been embarrassed as hell.

I still was.

And now Deke was standing in front of me, holding me captive, ready to embarrass me some more. And what's worse? He had Liam McCellan, Roselyn Bell, Ramsey Reed, and Emerson Andrews at his back, protecting him. They were his cover for whatever it was he wanted to do or say to me, and everyone knew not to mess with this crew. Ramsey Reed was a psychopath and Liam McCellan was as unstable as they came. And Liam was the nice one, for Christ's sake.

My little push to Deke's chest hadn't moved him a bit, and he stepped closer-if that was possible-and leaned down before saying, "Now, why would I want to do that?"

"I'm sorry, okay?" I mumbled. Maybe that's all he was looking for. "I won't tell any-"

Deke threw his head back in a sinister laugh. He looked back down at me and said, "You think I give a fuck if these people know that I just got my dick sucked?" *Evidently, not.* "Do you think Melissa Randall's virtue is so pristine that we need to protect her reputation?"

Oh, my God! What a jerk!

"Then what do you want," I asked through gritted teeth. I may be a nerd, but I wasn't a pushover.

"Delaney, what's going on?"

I sidestepped Deke to look beyond his tall body to see Ave standing behind Deke's little band of lunatics. She was standing behind, but in between, Liam and Roselyn. Good choice. The entire town knew Ramsey lost his mind anytime anyone came too close to Emerson. "Noth...nothing, Av-"

Deke tilted his head back and addressed Ava in a voice loud enough for everyone who was nearby to hear. The party around us had already quieted down when they took notice of Deke grabbing me and pushing me up against the car, so he didn't have to raise his voice all that much for Ava to hear him. "Mind your own business, Ava. This is between me and Delaney," he warned her.

My eyes left Ava's and when I looked back at Deke, his head was still tilted back and I could see the muscle and veins corded in his neck, and I swear to God, I wanted to latch onto him like a vampire. The realization made me tremble.

I was scared.

I'd never felt this way before, and I didn't need to feel this way about Deke Marlow. My arranged future husband, Winston Reynolds, was the only boy who should evoke these feelings in me.

NOT Deke Marlow.

"Leave me alone, Deke," I whispered, terrified of these new urges. So terrified, his head came down and his green eyes snapped to mine, because he could hear the fright in my voice.

And if I thought I was terrified before, that was nothing compared to the cold feeling in my bones when Deke leaned so close, his breath tickled my lips. "Not on your fucking life am I going to leave you alone now," he growled so low that only I could hear him.

I don't know how I did it, but I could see through his green gaze that I had awoken something in him that should never be awake.

I think I just became Deke Marlow's newest prey.

"Deke, leave her alone," Ava called out, and I had to give her credit. I didn't doubt her friendship, but no one-and I mean *no one*-went up against Deke, Liam, or Ramsey.

"Ava, this isn't your business, so just turn right back around and go on about whatever you were doing," Liam's voice snapped through the night.

I already had Deke's spotlight on me, I didn't need anyone going after Ava. Without taking my eyes off Deke, I called out to her. "It's okay, Ava.

Everything's fine. You can, uhm, go back to Marcos."

"But-"

"Ramsey…" Emerson's voice carried loud and clear.

I couldn't see it because Deke's large frame was blocking everything out, but I could hear Ramsey just as clearly as everyone else could. "Back off, Ava. *Now.*"

You could feel the shift in the air; the panic in the winds, the danger from the crackling bonfire. Emerson Andrews had just invoked her power over Ramsey Reed, and that was all she wrote, folks.

Ramsey had just handed me over to Deke Marlow without even knowing what he wanted me for. Actually, I suppose it was Emerson who handed me over to Deke. She's the one who called on Ramsey, after all.

I searched Deke's eyes looking for any signs of compassion, but there was nothing. "Don't do this, Deke," I begged. "Just…let me be. I'm sorry I watched yo-" His hand shot out, wrapping around my neck, and I did the worst thing I could have possibly done.

I moaned.

Darkness surfaced in his eyes, and that pulsing between my legs throbbed painfully. Deke squeezed his fingers around my neck, and it was everything I could do not to close my eyes and just bask in the force of his touch and the heat radiating off his body.

But I didn't.

"I'm going to let you go this time, Lamb," he whispered. "But I will be coming for you."

CHAPTER 3

Deke ~

"So, you going to finally tell us what's going on between you and Delaney Martin?" Liam asked as he and Ramsey walked into my game room. I didn't bother looking away from the 98" plasma screen television where I was currently battling the forces of darkness for all of mankind.

Last night after I let Delaney escape, Liam and Ramsey had kept mum because, while they loved the shit out of Emerson and Roselyn, they still respected my privacy. That's why they had formed a shield behind me when they saw something was up. It was that same sense of loyalty that had the girls standing next to them. They were loyal to Liam and Ramsey, hence, making them loyal to me.

Ramsey sat in his game chair positioned near the center table, while Liam dropped his body next to me on the black leather couch. I elbowed him because I knew it was a dick move to try to jam my game up. He scooted over as he laughed.

I shook my head, but grinned. Liam, Ramsey, and I have been friends all our lives, and I knew these two twisted fuck like I knew the back of my hand. And, while they might be twisted, they were loyal as fuck and, except for the girls, neither had a weak bone in their bodies.

Ramsey's father was a financier with Mob ties, so Ramsey's family was super wealthy, and that was saying something considering. His father was also shady as fuck and expected Ramsey to follow in his footsteps. Little did he know Ramsey already became his own man at the tender age of 15-years-old. Ramsey's life plans did not include his father or being anyone's little bitch; and that included the Mafia. And where Ramsey's father was a dick, his mother was just absent. She ran around doing who knows what, and no one ever asked.

Liam's parents were no better. His father managed a hedge fun for legitimate purposes but was just as shady with side-dealings as Ramsey's father. He was also an absolute asshole. Whereas Ramsey's father knew Ramsey was psychotic, and my father was nonexistent, Liam's father contacted him often just to be a dick to him. And Liam's mother did what most the wives of Sands Cove did-nothing. She was a vapid, self-absorbed idiot with too much money at her disposal.

I supposed that's why Ramsey was so fascinated with Emerson, and Liam was so wrapped up in Roselyn. These girls were the complete opposite of the kind of women they grew up despising.

As for me, my father worked in oil and energy solutions, but he was as crooked as a boxer's nose. There wasn't a bribe he ever refused and there wasn't a tramp he hadn't bedded. Sampson Marlow was a jackass of a peacock, always on stage and performing to impress. He was arrogant, vain, and just plain ridiculous. But he had the sleazy charm of a used car salesman and people ate it up.

My mother was another despicable human who paired with my father beautifully. She played the ignorant wife role to perfection, but she was anything but. The woman was worthless and would sell someone's baby if it meant another diamond on her finger.

Fucking people were horrible.

Too bad for us, their neglect and lack of basic human decency affected us growing up.

We were fucking horrible people too.

At least, we had been until Ramsey fell in love with Emerson, and Liam finally claimed Roselyn for himself. They were still heartless, fearless assholes, but softer, and I couldn't be happier for them. They found the Holy Grail. They were horrible and ruthless, but they managed to find the two females on the planet that could rein all that in. They were more human now that they had the girls.

Me?

I had the ability to care, as evident by my relationships with Ramsey, Liam, Roselyn, and Emerson, but the rest of the world? The rest of the world could suck my dick.

Well…the rest of the world except Delaney Martin, apparently.

Ramsey and Liam had picked up their remote controls and joined in on the game as I answered Liam. "She caught me getting my dick sucked by Melissa Randall behind the trees last night."

"Caught?" Ramsey said, asking for clarification.

"Well, not caught," I corrected. "I'm not sure what she was doing because I hadn't asked, but all I know is that in the middle of Melissa blowing me, I had heard a noise, and when I looked over, Delaney was standing behind a tree watching."

"What was she even doing at the party?" Liam asked, not really expecting an answer. "That girl never parties. Fuck, I don't think I've ever seen her outside of school or a goddamn library. Even as fucked up as Ava is, she's never dragged Delaney's along with her to a party."

"Speaking of Ava...what was all that about with Emerson, Ram?" I asked.

Ramsey laughed. "Emerson said she's never seen you react to a girl that way before, and she wanted to see how things were going to play out. She hadn't wanted Ava ending the show before it got started. She's rooting for Delaney."

Liam laughed, and I joined in. Most people would believe that Emerson might have been being a jealous girl because Ramsey's fucked Ava before, but there was one thing Emerson Andrews was not, and that was jealous over other girls. Not only did Emerson have no reservations about kicking someone's ass, she didn't have an ounce of insecurity regarding Ramsey intentions towards her.

"So, what's the plan?" Liam asked, as Ramsey added, "Yeah, what do you need from us?"

And that said it all.

They had no idea what I wanted with Delaney Martin, but that didn't matter. They were on my side no matter what I wanted with the girl. "I'm...intrigued," I answered truthfully.

"I bet," Ramsey laughed.

"Just like Liam pointed out," I went on, "the girl has never been to a party. Even as wild as her best friend is, Delaney's never been to a party or run amok. The first time she attends one of Sands Cove's teenage parties, she wanders off and has no qualms about watching me get my dick sucked? She's quiet, demure, and timid, but she was comfortable enough to leave Ava and wander off at her first party, *and* brave enough to watch me get head?" I shook my head. "There's more to that girl than I ever thought, and now, I'm curious."

Liam chuckled. "Good luck, man. I think you're going to need it."

His words resonated in my head, but I knew I wasn't going to need it. I wanted Delaney, and I'd have her; simple as that. "I don't need luck," I countered. "Who at Windsor is going to stop me?"

"So, it's like that?" Ramsey asked.

Fuck it.

We weren't big on secrets, and they deserved the truth if they were going to back me-which I knew they would. "When I had her up against the car, I wrapped my hand around her neck, and when I squeeze, she moaned," I divulged.

Liam let out a whoop. "Oh, man," he said gleefully, "that girl is so fucked."

Now, while I've wrapped my hand around a girl's throat before during sex, they expected it. They were those types of girls. They wanted dirty, rough sex. As much as sex was just a physical release for me, I wasn't a complete asshole. I paid attention to the girl and made sure she got off and enjoyed herself. If I ever got the vibe that a girl wasn't into choking, biting, or bruises...well, then

I just fucked her easy-peasy style and sent her on her way.

Delaney wasn't supposed to have liked that squeeze around her neck. Everything I've ever known about her suggested she'd get scared. That threat to her safety should have brought on pleas, tears, and apologies.

But it hadn't.

The girl had moaned, and I had been ready to mount her right there against the car in front of every-goddamn-body.

While Liam was laughing at my predicament, Ramsey was more thoughtful; more insightful. "So, she's the one, huh?"

Was she?

I wasn't sure. But what I did know was that I've never had an emotional reaction to a girl like that before. Sure, I got turned on, and I hated tears, but the anxiousness Delaney made me feel was new.

I had to tug my dick to the memory of her body pressed up against mine last night, and again, this morning. "I'm not sure, Ram," I admitted. "But nothing's going to stop me from finding out if she is or isn't."

"Do we tell the girls?" Liam asked. "I mean…they need to know, right?"

I thought about that, and he was right. Emerson and Roselyn were my family now, and they deserved the same respect as Ramsey and Liam. "Yeah, but make sure they know not to interfere," I answered. Nothing and no one would stop me from going after Delaney to see if this was real or not.

Ramsey snorted. "I'm pretty sure them girls will be setting up a betting pool by the end of the week. No way they'll interfere."

I laughed because, knowing Roselyn and Emerson, he was probably right. "Tell them to bet wisely, because I will win," I joked.

"Never doubted it, Deke," Ramsey said.

CHAPTER 4

Delaney ~

I was a coward.

Okay, maybe not a *coward,* so much as a wimp.

Okay, okay, okay…I was a coward; proven by the fact that I've barricaded myself in my room and have turned off all notification on my phone because all everyone's been talking about on social media is Deke's…uh, interest in me last night.

And why wouldn't it be news? Deke effin' Marlow chased me down and held me hostage in front of everyone. And I knew it was the chasing that had garnered all the attention.

Deke Marlow never chased *anyone.*

Even if I have never been a part of the royal hierarchy, Deke's, Ramsey's, and Liam's reputations preceded them. They had never been short of female companionship, and if the rumors were to be believed, before Emerson and Roselyn came into the picture, all three guys were hit-it-and-quit-it kind of guys. They could have any girl they wanted, so it made no sense that Deke would single me out. By all accounts, I was the very definition of a nerd.

I never went to parties. I never drank. I've never touched a drug in my life. I didn't go on shopping sprees or live lavishly, even though I had the money to do it. I think being raised by the cook, butler, gardener, etc. gave me a grounded upbringing. I saw how hard they worked for their paychecks, and that always stuck with me. As for boys…well, I always knew I was going to marry Winston Reynolds. Our parents had broken the news to us when we were like 10-years-old, or something like that.

My father, Jonah Martin, worked in pharmaceuticals and Winston's father, Gary Reynolds, worked with insurance of some sort. Together they made a lot of money off sick people, and their greed never ran out of thirst. My mother, Shirley, was the perfect charitable socialite, whereas Winston's mother had run off with the pool boy or something years ago. As far as I knew, she took off and never looked back.

I didn't mind not having my parents around, though. They were horrible human beings, and the less time I spent with them, the less likely they'd rub off on me. I learned early on they weren't nice people, especially when they had scarred my face using the excuse as medical research as the reason.

It was before we had moved to Sands Cove and my father was still trying to make a name for himself. He had helped develop a scar erasing serum that had made it possible for us to go from Upper-Class America to the One-Percent.

I could remember it like it was yesterday. I had been 6-years-old and I remember how my father and mother had held me down and ran a barbed wire across my face, slicing it open. I remembered all the blood. I remembered the pain-*God*, did I remember the pain. I remembered feeling the jagged edges of my skin hanging on my face. I remembered my parents discussing my injury with such detachment. My mother promised that they'd get the best plastic surgeon in the world to help me, but for now, I had to help the family.

The joke had been on them, though.

My father's plan had been to use my face and the hook of me being his daughter to promote his serum. However, I had had such a horrible allergic reaction to some of the properties in the serum, it actually burned my flesh. While the serum has works for million others, I had been part of the small percent that suffered the rare side effects of the potion.

I remember being six and feeling ecstatic at how it hadn't worked for me. My parents hadn't deserved for it to work on me after what they did to me. As the years went by, and I realized how truly horrible my parents were, I declined plastic surgery options because I wanted them to have to look at me and see the evidence of what horrible people they were.

Not that they cared, but still.

Shortly after moving here, my parents had met the Reynolds, and a love affair was born out of my father's need for accolades, and Mr. Reynolds greed for money. It wasn't long before they concocted the match between their children to help further their agendas. Winston's stepmother pushed for it-*hard*.

At the time, I hadn't known what all of that had meant, but as I got older and knew what they were about, I hadn't been too interested in alternatives to fight them on it. Besides, the marriage was to take place after Winston and I graduated from college. A lot could happen in four years when we're both away from each other and we're thrust into the arms of real life. Winston might find another match better suited for his family's needs.

He could also get hit by a bus.

Or I could.

But, being betrothed hadn't stopped him from losing his virginity to Clair McDaniels. It also hasn't stopped him from sleeping with any willing girl at

Windsor. I suppose it should bother me, but I couldn't garner enough energy or emotions to care what Winston Reynolds did. He was *that* inconsequential.

The door to my bedroom flew open, and I didn't even need to look up from my tablet to know who it was. Because I was a dork, I didn't have many friends. And the friends I did have wouldn't just barge into my house.

I felt Ava's weight drop on my bed as she said, "Okay, I let you flee from the party last night like a bat out of hell because I knew you were trippin' out, and truth be told, so was I. But you gotta come clean now, chic. I let you sleep in and everything, but no more."

I sighed and put down my tablet, knowing she wasn't going to go anywhere until she got the goods. "There's nothing to come clean about, Ava," I denied.

She rolled over onto her side and propped her head up over her hand. "You randomly take off from the party, and not twenty minutes later, you come rushing back with Deke Marlow hot on your tail as you grab me and beg for us to leave," she recited. "That's not nothing, Delaney."

It didn't feel right telling her what I saw, but if she was going to stick by me like she did last night, she should know the facts. "I was just…wandering around, and I got kind of lost. When I found a tiny clearing, I saw Deke getting a blowjob from Melissa Randall."

Ava's brows rose up casually. "So? Melissa Randall's blown a lot of people," she pointed out, making me feel like an even bigger nerd. Ava's never teased me or made me feel stupid for being a virginal nerd, but sometimes I felt ridiculous discussing sex with someone so experienced. I felt inferior.

"I think Deke took exception to me…seeing it happen," I hedged.

Ava let out a laugh as she dropped onto her back. She laughed up at the ceiling as she said, "Oh, please, Delaney. Deke Marlow does not care about someone watching him get a blowjob." I could feel the blush rush my face at her casualness. "I've been to countless parties where that dude got his dick sucked in public. I mean, he didn't drop his pants in the middle of a living room or anything like that, but there have been plenty of times he was huddled up in a corner somewhere with a girl on her knees in front of him." *Jesus.* "Trust me, Delaney, whatever was bothering him last night, that was not it."

"Then I don't know what his problem was," I told her half-ass honestly. "Maybe he was just funnin' about."

This time she snorted. "Deke Marlow doesn't fun about, Delaney. The guy's Satan."

"I thought Ramsey Reed was Satan?"

"Good point," she quipped. A few seconds of silence went by before she said, "What are you going to tell Winston?"

Huh?

"Nothing," I replied. "There's nothing to tell him. Besides, if I were to ride Deke Marlow in the middle of the eatery pavilion at school Monday, Winston would hardly have any room to complain, don'tcha think?"

Ava sat up and side-eyed me. "I still can't believe you have an arranged marriage with that tool."

I shrugged a shoulder. "Families with money do it all the time, Ava. How many people with money ever really marry for love? Most females from our class marry for more money and most males from our class marry for more power. It's not that unrealistic."

"But you couldn't care less about money or power, Delaney," she murmured softly. "Don't tie yourself to a fool for life just because you haven't experienced anything worthwhile yet."

I looked over at my friend and wondered, not for the first time, if she had been sexually abused as a child. I couldn't reconcile this sweet, tender girl with the sexually wild party girl. "I still have four years to either go through with this or bow out, Ava," I reminded her. "It's not forever, yet."

The corner of her lip lifted in a mischievous grin. "If you're going to go through with this ridiculous betrothal, I say you take Deke Marlow for a ride first before committing to Winston for life."

I wanted to scoff at how ridiculous that suggestion was, but I couldn't when her statement held a grain of truth to it. It had crossed my mind. Watching Deke and Melissa had turned me on. Getting caught had really lit a fire between my legs. But when Deke chased me down and wrapped his hand around my neck, all kinds of things I never imagined crossed through my mind. For the first time in all my life, I had wanted to have sex with someone.

No-not *someone*; Deke.

During those early puberty years, I had let Winston kiss me, but I never felt anything, and so, I put a stop to those kisses.

But Deke wasn't Winston.

CHAPTER 5

Deke ~

I watched Delaney and Ava walk past our little group, like I have for the past four years, but this time was different. This time I *saw* them walking past our group.

Every morning for the past four years, Ramsey, Liam, and I had always congregated around our cars in the parking lot in front of the school before classes began. We were always surrounded by random stragglers, but for the most part, it was me, Ram, and Liam. Emerson and Roselyn would often loiter with us too, but there *were* rare days where Liam and Ramsey let them do their own thing. And now sitting on the hood of my Lexus, I appeared casual, but I'd been looking to spot Delaney since I got here.

I spent all day yesterday straight up stalking her social media, and all my stalking accomplished was confirming that the girl didn't have a life. It appeared as if she lived vicariously through Ava's antics, because all her pictures were either of school stuff or girl time with Ava. There were random pictures of her posted with other people who I presumed might be family, but since I didn't know much about Delaney, I really had no idea who those people were.

I did note a couple of family-looking pictures with Winston Reynolds, and that had surprised me a bit because I had never seen them act chummy at all. Granted, I wasn't friends with Winston, and I never really paid any attention to Delaney before Friday night, but I just never imagined they were friends.

Delaney and I had second, third, and seventh periods together, so I was going to have to let her be during first period, but she'd be all mine during second. I'd have to share her with Linnie during third, but Delaney would be all mine again during seventh. It's not that I thought Linnie wouldn't back my play, but girls were funny sometimes. And don't get me started on when it's that time of the month. Talk about dealing with the devil you don't know.

Sweet Baby Jesus.

Looking over at Delaney, I ignored the pull that called on me to run after her, and stayed my ass planted on the hood of my car. It wasn't a second later I abandoned that plan when Ramsey smirked at me. If anyone knew what I was feeling, it was Ramsey. Emerson just about drove him crazy those first few weeks of their fucked-up courtship. I hopped off my hood and took off in a sprint; a sprint that didn't go unnoticed, might I add.

Luckily, I had everything I needed for first period in my backpack, so I could skip my locker. I headed straight to where I knew Delaney's locker was. And how did I know were her locker was? Sunday, while I was internet stalking her, I had texted Ramsey to get me all her school information, and he did. I knew the guy could get information on damn near anyone he wanted, so by Sunday evening, I had her class schedule, her locker number, her phone number, her parents' names and professions, her address, and he even threw in her favorite book, just to show off.

The fucker.

I was walking up behind her, and because I was indeed a lucky guy, Ava's locker was nowhere near Delaney's, so there was no one to interrupt my good morning greeting.

The locker door was opened on my side, so she couldn't see me coming and that had my dick twitching with anticipation of her reaction. I stepped up behind her and gave her no room to escape. I brushed my body up against hers, and my dick got instantly hard when her entire body stilled. She had been in the middle of pulling a book out of her locker, and her entire body absolutely froze.

I leaned down and let my lips brush up against the shell of her ear. "Good Morning, Delaney," I said, my voice low for only her to hear.

"Wh…what are you doing?" she asked, and my dick got even harder at the hitch in her voice.

"Saying hello," I smirked.

She didn't respond. She went about finishing pulling her book out of her locker. I imagined she was trying to buy herself some time to figure out how to proceed. When she finally did turn around, my dick and I were both disappointed that he was no longer nestled near her ass.

Delaney looked up at me, and she looked irritated. I had been expecting some apprehensiveness, maybe a little fear, but I had gotten irritation instead. "Leave me alone, Deke," she instructed, trying to sound strong and firm.

I grinned and shook my head. "Not a chance in hell of that happening, Delaney. So, don't waste your energy on that."

Her eyes darted around, taking in the crowd taking notice of our proximity, before landing back on mine. "I said I was sorry," she hissed. "I'll never invade your privacy again, so just leave me alone."

I reached up, and it was game on when my fingertips danced across her scar and she didn't recoil. I was going to fuck this girl. I was going to use up everything she had to offer. I was going to fucking *own* her. If she had any clue what I was going to do to her, she run, and she'd run far.

The second warning bell for class rang, and the students around us still didn't scatter to get to class. Everyone was watching, and I wasn't going to let them go without something to talk about. I cupped her jaw in my hand, and I did something I've never done with a girl before outside of fucking her. I leaned down and kissed Delaney on her cupid-bowed lips. She gasped, and I used that shock to sweep my tongue in her mouth, tighten my hold on her face, and kiss the fuck out of her. And this first kiss gave me an answer to take back to Ramsey and Liam.

She was the one.

Delaney Martin was my Emerson and Roselyn, and the girl had no clue what that meant.

All too soon, Delaney's shock wore off, and she pushed me off her, and the slap that followed surprised her just as much as it surprised everyone else. I'm not sure what surprised her more, the slap or the force behind the slap, but when I turned back to face her, she looked equal parts shocked and pissed off.

I wanted to fuck her right here and now in front of everyone.

Delaney hugged her book to her chest in a white-knuckle grip. "You...you don't..." she was so upset she couldn't even speak. "You don't just get to kiss me, Deke!"

I threw my head back and let out a dark laugh. I looked back down at her, and in a voice the entire hallway could hear, I announced, "You're mine, Delaney. I get to do whatever the fuck I want to you."

You could hear gasps and murmurs all around us, but they weren't as loud as Delaney's gasp of outrage. "I'm...I'm *not* yours," she seethed. "I don't even *like* you!"

This time, in a voice low enough for only her and a few close students to hear, I growled, "You ask anyone in this school an hour from now and they will all say you belong to *me*, Delaney. Give in gracefully, baby, otherwise, this could get ugly."

"Are you threatening me?" she asked, and I had to give the girl credit; she was a lot braver than I ever imagined she'd be. Quiet, demure Delaney Martin was showing me her hidden sides, and by the time I was done with her, I'd know them all.

I rubbed the sting on my face and she had the grace to flush a bit at the action. I knew she surprised herself with such a violent reaction to my kiss, but all that did was show me that she wasn't fragile. She wasn't delicate. And all that meant was that I didn't have to treat her with kid gloves once I got her naked.

I was going to ruin this girl.

I was going to ruin her for every other man on the planet. She was mine, and once I tell Ramsey, Liam, Emerson, and Roselyn, there'd be nowhere for her to hide.

The third, and final, bell for class rang, and I knew no one would go to class as long as this little drama was still playing out, so I leaned down-risking another slap to the face-placed a kiss on her cheek and winked at her before taking off to my first period.

The teacher didn't question me when I arrived to class late. Mr. Stevens just continued on as if my arrival hadn't been a disruption. I noticed a couple of other kids had followed behind me, being late themselves because they had stuck around to watch the drama, but again, Mr. Stevens hadn't chastised anyone.

After I sat down and got situated, Meghan Swiftly leaned over towards me and whispered, "So, you and Delaney Martin, huh?"

I barked out a laugh because I had no doubt there was a video on someone's phone of that epic slap that was now circulating the classroom. That fact was confirmed a second later when my phone chimed with a text from Liam with a laughing emoji, a text from Ramsey asking if I was okay, a text from Emerson that just said 'wow', and a text from Linnie using the same laughing emoji Liam had sent.

Fucking assholes.

Instead of texting back those insensitive assholes, I looked over at Meghan and answered, "Yeah, me and Delaney Martin."

Meghan didn't shy away from getting into my business. "That slap looked pretty vicious," she pointed out.

Yeah, it was. "Does it matter?" I asked, not really expecting an answer. Meghan knew what I was getting at, and it'd be all over school within minutes.

She shook her head. "I suppose not."

CHAPTER 6

Delaney ~

First period had been horrible, and knowing that Deke was in my second, third, and seventh periods, I was confident the rest of the day was going to be worse.

And, Christ, did I really slap Deke Marlow in front of everyone?

Why, yes. Yes, I did, if the video along with a 'WTF?' text from Ava was any indication. I didn't have Ava in any classes until fourth period, but we usually saw each other in passing on our way to class. I looked down at my phone as it vibrated with another text from her. As entitled as we were, most of us respected the classroom rules of phones on silent. When the administration knew they couldn't fight the battle of no phones at all, they had compromised and as long as our phones were on silent, the teachers didn't fight us. The only time phones were not allowed out was during testing.

WTF?

Is this real, Delaney?

Oh, how I wish I could text her back no.

Unfortunately

Her reply came immediately.

Holy Moly!

I stifled my laugh. The girl was as wild as they came, and she texted that. Before I could text back, another one from her came through.

U bttr tell W about D! Or D about W!

I didn't think it was necessary to tell Winston about Deke or the other way around. Winston didn't have a leg to stand on regarding if I messed around with other guys, and Deke…well, Winston wasn't any of Deke's business.

Explain ltr.

I sat through class ignoring the only other text that had come through a few minutes later.

B waiting by ur locker aftr class or else.

I hadn't even bothered myself with wondering how Deke got my number. Even if he couldn't get it, everyone in town knew Ramsey Reed had connections the CIA would envy. I had no doubt that whatever information Deke couldn't find about me on his own, Ramsey would have gotten for him.

The bell rang after forty minutes of feeling like an exhibition animal at the zoo, but I knew next period would be the same. Hell, it would be worse because Deke would be in there with me. I ignored all the stares and rumblings as I made my way to my locker-and *not* because Deke had commanded it. I had to go get my stupid calculus book.

I cursed his gorgeous face as he leaned up against my locker with his arms crossed over his chest, a stupid smirk on his face. He stepped out of the way as soon as I stood in front of him and waited patiently as I unlocked my locker to get switch books. "Go away, Deke," I muttered. Why he was still playing this game after I slapped him was beyond me.

"I already told you, Delaney. That's not happening," he replied.

I shut my locker and turned around to face the asshole. "Why?" I demanded. "Why are you fucking with me?"

He smirked, and as God as my witness, I wanted to slap the shit out of him again. "I haven't even *begun* to fuck with you, Delaney."

I had been afraid of that.

Deke has been bolder than most, but I knew his antics so far haven't even begun to scratch the surface of what he was capable. Right now, he was just teasing me. He was a deadly cat playing with a nerdy mouse. He was just waiting for me to do that one thing that would excuse him to go in for the kill.

"Why?" I asked again. This had to be about more than me just watching him get a blowjob. If what Ava said was true, he shouldn't care this much about voyeurism.

He leaned down into my face, and I knew the people around us would *kill* to hear what we were saying. "Because you moaned," he said, confirming my worst fears. "You moaned like a bitch in heat when I had my hand wrapped around your neck and I *knew*. I knew you'd let me fuck you right then and there in front of everyone had I tried." I stayed stubbornly mute because I didn't trust my voice to sound strong enough and convincing enough to deny it. "I thought you spent all these years saving yourself because you were a good girl, but that's not it at all. You're still a virgin because you're too scared to voice what you want."

"Ho...how do you know I'm even a virgin?" I challenged. I couldn't do anything about the roughness in my voice, but I wanted to know. "How do you know I haven't slept with anyone already?"

His green eyes were looking right through the façade I was doing my best to project. "Because you wouldn't have looked so needy when you were watching me get my dick sucked, Delaney. And if you're not a virgin, then the guys you've been with haven't been satisfying you for shit."

The bell for class rang, and I thanked God. I wasn't equipped to have a conversation with Deke Marlow about sex. He was right. I was a virgin. He was also right about why. It was probably the reason no boys had ever caught my attention here. They were all too...soft. When you're handed everything you always want, where's the effort?

I decided not to comment on his observations, and I turned to head to class. Deke stepped in line with me and I was startled stupid when he reached for my hand to freakin' *hold* it. Shock and sheer pride had me snatching my hand back. I didn't know what Deke was about, but I wasn't going to willingly be a part of whatever bet or game he was playing at.

What happened next will stay with me forever.

One second, I was walking to class trying to wrap my mind around Deke's madness, and the next, my back was up against a wall with Deke looming over me. His eyes looked like green fire. "Understand something, Delaney, and it's in your best interest to comprehend and understand this immediately," he snarled. "I'm not Ramsey, and I'm not Liam."

I was terrified, but I'd be damned if I would show him any weakness. I *knew* I was the mouse. "What does th...that mean?"

Deke looked positively lethal when he said, "It means, I'm not Liam who has been in love with Roselyn since forever, and I'm not Ramsey who gave Emerson a choice." *Holy shit.* "It means if I say you're fucking mine, then. You. Are. Mine. Don't ever pull away from me again."

"You can't do this, Deke," I cried. "You can't just...just..." I was sputtering like a fool because he wasn't making any sense. He's ignored me for four years and, suddenly, he's claiming me and proclaiming it as law?

"Who's going to stop me?" he asked, and I had no answer to that.

Who would stop him? Winston? My parents? Winston's parents? The law? The law could stop him, right? If everyone else failed, a restraining order would surely shut this madness down, right?

My mind scrambled for some kind of solution to my situation. It was one thing to tease me about sex; it was another to hold my hand in the hallway on our way to class. That hinted at shit that he couldn't possibly want with me. I knew I wasn't a complete toad, but I wasn't powerful like Emerson or strong like Roselyn, and Deke Marlow needed a girl with a commanding presence to walk with him in that context. His group of friends wouldn't tolerate a weak link, and I would totally be a weak link.

Maybe...

"I'll make you a deal," I whispered. He didn't comment. He just arched an ebony brow. "I'll let you..." *Christ,* I couldn't believe I was even contemplating this, much less saying it out loud. "...be my first. I'll let you...have your way, but then after that, you leave me alone." *Take away the curiosity, right?*

"Oh, I'm going to be your first, alright," he smirked. "I'm going to be your last, too. And I had better be your only, Delaney." I stared dumbfounded as he said, "Let's get to class."

Ava was right.

I was going to have to tell him about Winston.

CHAPTER 7

Deke ~

I've never tried to hold a girl's hand before, and so, Delaney's blatant rejection had had me seeing red like a sonofabitch. I had been so pissed when we finally got to class, I had dragged her with me towards the back of the stadium seating and planted her ass next to mine.

I'll admit that this had all started out as curiosity, but that kiss changed everything.

I've kissed plenty of girls in my lifetime, but the kisses had all been part of foreplay. I never kissed a girl who I wasn't about to fuck, and I sure as fuck have never kissed a girl in public for the sake of demonstrating affection. Hell, I've never even had a girlfriend before. I didn't need one, and sex around here was served on goddamn tap. I didn't need to a girlfriend to get laid.

But Delaney Martin had changed all that with that kiss and that goddamn slap afterwards.

Even though I wasn't a psychopath like Ramsey, or a madman like Liam, my tastes had always run towards the darker side of things. I was fine with soft sex and missionary if that's what the girl preferred, but what I preferred was hard, rough fucking. I enjoyed pulling on a girl's hair so hard it brought tears to her eyes. I enjoyed leaving bite marks and bruises. I enjoyed the ownership. I enjoyed knowing a girl was so out of her mind with pleasure that pain didn't register. I loved knowing that a girl was so turned on she'd let me do whatever I wanted to her.

Admittedly, throughout my eighteen years of life, I've only experienced that a few times, and it was with one-night-stands from other towns or some of the older siblings of the girls I went to school with. Not too many teenage girls will let a guy choke the shit out of her during sex.

But I saw that...desire on Delaney's face when she focused on my hands tightening in Melissa's hair Friday night. I saw that same curious need on her face when she slapped me. And I saw it in her eyes when I explained how I knew she was a virgin.

Anticipation nearly drove me to my knees at the thought of Delaney bleeding all over me. I never knew why Liam had deceived Roselyn the night he took her virginity and did it without a condom on, but now that I've…connected with Delaney, well, now I understood. I wanted my dick covered in the proof that she's never been with anyone else. Birth control was something we were going to have to discuss because, the way I'm feeling now, I wouldn't care if she got pregnant.

And, right now, my future-baby-mamma was reluctantly being dragged behind me as we walked to my locker so I could pick up Linnie for third period. It astounded me sometimes how I could have had sex with Roselyn for close to a year and still feel nothing but friendship for her. It's only been a few months since the last time I saw her naked, but I can't even picture her anymore, and not because she wasn't memorable. My mind tricked my memories somehow the second she became exclusive with Liam.

We walked up to my locker and since all our lockers were together, with the exception of Linnie's, all my friends were standing gathered around. Liam had second period with Roselyn, so he turned her over to me during third and fourth periods, and then he got her back during fifth. Emerson and Roselyn always had one of us with them. The only exception was Roselyn's sixth period. She was alone, but it was art, so she was allowed to wander around taking pictures and shit if she wanted to. Liam couldn't get her scheduled changed so late in the year.

And all of our possessiveness was simply due to the fact that even as tough as our girls were, there were plenty of people still hating on them for doing the one thing they couldn't; landing Ramsey and Liam. Thinking about it, I knew I was going to see what I could do about Delaney's schedule now.

The second we stopped in front of my friends, Liam fired the first shot. "That's a hell of a swing," he chuckled. "Did you have to go see the nurse?"

I opened my locker with the one hand that held Delaney's. No way would I let go of her hand. She'd take off running. "Fuck you, dude," I replied, putting my book away and grabbing another.

"Hi, Delaney," Emerson said, greeting her. "I don't think we've ever been formally introduced."

"Very polite, babe," Roselyn laughed.

Emerson side-eyed Roselyn. "What? I don't want the girl to think we're *all* crazy."

I rolled my eyes as Delaney addressed Emerson. "It doesn't matter, Emerson," she replied. "I'm not going to be around long enough for it to matter."

You could hear a pin drop.

Ramsey's and Liam's eyes shot to mine, while the girls looked uncomfortably everywhere else but at me or Delaney. I slammed my locker shut, letting the noise cut through the tense silence. "Keep talking that shit,

Delaney, and see what happens."

The strength in her voice surprised me. I thought being around everyone would intimidate her, but it didn't. "You can say whatever you want, and act like an asshole however much you want, but that changes nothing, Deke," she announced before cutting to the heart of the issue. Most girls would kill to date me, but her next words told me everything I needed to know about her reluctance. "You've ignored me for four years. You can just keep on ignoring me."

She was right.

I never paid her any mind. I never thought about her. I never spoke to her. She never even crossed my mind whenever I did see her passing in the hallway, or wherever. I had lumped her in with the masses, and now that she had my attention, she was throwing it back in my face, and I really couldn't fault the girl.

"Delaney?" Every head swiveled to see Ava standing a few feet away, clearly concerned for her friend, but not confident enough to approach us all. While Ava had a spine of steel and wasn't timid in the least, there's no way she was brave enough to battle me, Liam, and Ramsey. She also knew that the fact that she's slept with both Ramsey and Liam, it'd be up to the girls if she was ever welcomed into our fold.

Delaney yanked her hand out of mine, and without a word, turned her back on us and rushed towards her friend. I let her go because it wasn't like I didn't know where to find her. We had our next class together.

After they were out of earshot, Ramsey asked, "Trouble?"

"She offered to let me be her first if I promised to leave her the hell alone afterwards," I admitted. Liam let out a low whistle and the girls both visibly winced.

"Uh, that doesn't sound promising, Deke," Roselyn pointed out unnecessarily.

"Especially after that slap heard around the world," Emerson added.

I looked over at my two pretty girls. "Doesn't matter," I told them. "She's mine."

"What do you need from us until she comes to terms with that?" Ramsey asked.

"Just watch out for her if I'm not around," I answered, even though I knew that was a given with them.

The bell rang, and I grabbed Linnie's hand and dragged her with me to third period. I'd miss Delaney during fourth period, but after fourth it'd be lunchtime, and I expected Delaney to be sitting with us at our table. When we got to class, I saw that Delaney was sitting in the front between two other girls. There was no room for me or Roselyn and that wasn't acceptable.

As Roselyn marched towards the back where we always sat, I walked over three students until I was standing next to Delaney. I grabbed her backpack and book off the desk with one hand while my other hand wrapped around the back of her neck. I squeezed and pulled her out of her seat literally dragging her struggling and cussing through the row of students.

"What the hell, Deke?" she yelled. I ignored her as I walked her up the steps towards the back.

"Mr. Marlow?"

I didn't bother looking back. It's not as if Mrs. Joy was going to interfere. "Delaney was lost, Mrs. Joy," I called back. "I'm just helping her find her way."

And then Delaney Martin really got my dick hard. "You motherfucker!" she ranted.

I took a seat, and with my hand still wrapped around her neck, I forced her to the seat next to me. Linnie was sat on my other side, wisely not saying anything. "Sit your ass down, Delaney," I snapped. "Sit the fuck down or I swear I will drag you out of this school and no one will hear from you all week."

Her bright brown eyes were shooting out sparks, but she wasn't stupid. She knew I could do what I just threatened and that no one would stop me. There's a chance Ava might, but I knew Delaney wouldn't want to put Ava on my bad side.

Delaney sat down and slammed her book on the desktop in a show of rage and defiance. She didn't bother to look at me when she said, "Go ahead and think you have me under control, Deke," she hissed. "But rest assured you do *not.*"

My arm shot out and snaked a fist full of her brown hair in my hand and I twisted her head towards me. I had my lips mashed to hers in a bruising, forceful kiss. She opened her mouth to let out a grimace at the pain, and the second she did, I bit down on her bottom lip until I tasted blood. The warmth that flooded my tongue made me damn near delirious with need.

I pulled back and, have you ever been so enraged that tears burned in your eyes? Well, right now, that was Delaney Martin. The look in her pretty brown eyes was pure unadulterated rage and hate for me, in this moment.

There was no way she was sleeping anywhere but in my bed with me. *Ever.*

CHAPTER 8

Delaney ~

In a surprise move, five minutes before the bell rang for fourth period, I had jumped out of my seat and ran out of the classroom before Deke could stop me. I ran out past the teacher and didn't stop until I was safely secured in the girl's restroom. Windsor had three different girls' restrooms, so I ran to the farthest one from class and Deke's locker.

It might have been cowardly to flee like that, but the rage I had been feeling all through class gave me no choice. It was either run or beat Deke Marlow within an inch of his life.

I knew the more I fought, the more it called onto his predatory instincts, but what else could I do? I wasn't going to just follow him blindly, nodding my head like a tool. Or maybe that's what I needed go do for him to lose interest.

When I had suggested I let him be my first as long as he left me alone afterwards, I had suggested that for a lot of reason. Even though I still had another four years to commit before I couldn't change my mind, if I married Winston, I planned on being faithful even if he wasn't. I might not be marrying him for love, but that didn't make marriage vows any less sacred. A part of me kept going over Ava's suggestion of having a fling with Deke before giving myself to Winston for life, but I wondered if I'd be better off not knowing what I was missing. I didn't suspect Winston would be horrible to me or even horrible in bed, Lord knows the boy's had enough practice if the rumors were to be believed, but I didn't *feel* anything with him. Winston didn't inspire any emotions out of me; not love, like, lust, excitement, anger, jealousy, warmth…*nothing.* And I had a feeling that if I let Deke in my bed, and then had to settle for Winston afterwards, I'd be sorely disappointed for the rest of my life.

"Delaney?"

I whirled around and there stood the guy occupying my thoughts.

31

"Winston," I breathed out. "This is the girls' restroom. What are you doing in here?"

He walked towards me until he was standing in front of me, looking down into my face. Winston was an attractive boy, with his dark brown hair and startling blue eyes, but he just did nothing for me. "I left class early so I could catch you by your locker and I saw you running this way."

"Let's go talk outside," I suggested. The bell had rung a few seconds ago and I knew girls would be coming in soon to use this restroom. He followed me outside and we kept walking until we found a little alcove on the side of the building. I pressed my back up against the wall and looked up at him. "Why were you going to wait for me?"

The look he gave me would have cut through a lesser person, and it gave me pause. In all the years I've known Winston, I've never seen him upset. This was new. "Why the hell do you think, Delaney?" he snapped. "There's a goddamn video of Deke Marlow kissing you and you slapping the shit out of him." I closed my eyes and sighed. When I reopened them, Winston's expression hadn't changed. He still looked pissed. "What the hell is going on between you and Deke Marlow?"

I dropped my backpack on the ground next to me and crossed my arms over my chest. "Nothing is going on between me and Deke," I denied. "And, even if there was, what business is it of yours?"

His dark brows shot up. "Are you serious? We're supposed to get married one day," he reminded me. "Anything you do is my goddamn business."

I laughed at that. "Are you serious?" I didn't let him answer. "You haven't made my life your business since the day I met you, Winston. And now, suddenly, you give a shit?"

"You've always been my business, Delaney," he repeated. "You've just never had any business to get into, until now." His eyes darted to my split lip; Deke's bite mark.

Wow.

Talk about some nerve. "So, suddenly, you're jealous?" I asked. "You've slept with half the school and you want to stake claim now that someone is showing me interest?"

His jaw ticked and I could tell he didn't like being called out on his behavior. "Delaney, if you wanted to spend your high school years sowing your wild oats, I would have understood. Just like you gave me the freedom I needed, I would have done the same," he said, lying through his teeth. "My problem is you wait until we're seniors, when our arrangement is getting closer, to start getting involved with other guys."

"Getting involved with other guys," I murmured. I cocked my head at him. "I'm not even involved with *you.*"

"Cut the shit, Delaney," he barked. "You know damn well what I mean. All those other girls? I made it clear I was unavailable for more than sex. Does Marlow know you're taken?"

I uncrossed my arms and ran my hands through my hair in frustration. "No," I told him. "He doesn't know because he doesn't need to know. There's nothing going on between us."

"That kiss suggests otherwise, Delaney," he argued.

I dropped my head back, closed my eyes, and let out a deep sigh. For four years I've been ignored by everyone, and in the span of a weekend and one crappy Monday, I had the attention of two guys I didn't know what to do with.

This fucking sucked.

I could hear and feel Winston step closer, and when I opened my eyes, he was towering over me, and I wished-*oh, God,* how I wished he did something for me. If he had, we would have begun a real relationship years ago, and I would have never had been at that stupid party and I never would have gotten caught in Deke's crosshairs.

The look of irritation was gone, but not forgotten. I needed to make a mental note that Winston wasn't as laid back as he seemed. He reached up and pushed a lock of hair behind my ear. It's the first time since the last time we kissed, when we were 14-years-old, that he's shown any affection towards me. "Delaney, you're mine," he stated. "You've always been mine no matter what...may have transpired over the years. You need to tell Deke."

"I couldn't agree more," came a voice that froze the both of us.

The bottom of my stomach fell out and I wouldn't have been surprised if I had fallen out in a full-blown panic attack. Winston turned around, and we were both face to face with Ramsey Reed. I was pretty sure I was going to be sick.

"Reed," Winston acknowledged.

"Reynolds," Ramsey acknowledged back.

I stepped forward, and the movement made Ramsey's eyes focus on mine. "Uhm..."

Ramsey threw up a hand to stop me. He looked back and forth between me and Winston as he said, "I'm going to make this short and sweet. Someone-I don't care who-better explain what I just walked up on and heard."

I had to give Winston credit. He stepped up and explained the situation. "Delaney and I are engaged to be married. The arrangement was made years ago by our parents, and we'll be getting married after we graduate from college." Ramsey's eyes shot to mine before returning to Winston's as he went on, "I was just making sure Delaney was...being honest about her situation."

Ramsey addressed Winston, "So, you're telling me that you and Delaney have an arranged marriage agreement, and you're just making sure she's not stringing Deke along, is that it?"

"Yeah. We...we agreed to get...some stuff out of our systems before committing to marriage, and since this is the first time Delaney's shown any, uhm, interest in anyone, I just wanted to make sure she was being forthcoming." I wanted to argue against Winston's explanation because he was half-ass lying, but I wasn't sure if I was up to going against Ramsey Reed, so I kept quiet.

Ramsey gave Winston a terse nod, as if he was mulling over Winston's words in his head. He finally cocked his head and told Winston, "Here's what's going to happen, Reynolds. You ever touch Delaney again while this thing with her and Deke is going on, you won't live to ever touch her again." I gasped, but Ramsey wasn't finished. "I don't care what plans you two have set for when you graduate college, but right here, right now, you will stay the fuck away from her until Deke tells you otherwise, got it?"

Ramsey didn't wait for Winston to agree or disagree. He walked over, grabbed my backpack off the ground, grabbed me by my arm and dragged me away.

Shit. This was bad.

Ramsey was literally dragging me behind him and wasn't even bothering to look at me as he spoke. "I have nothing against you, Delaney, so I'm doing you a favor here. You better tell Deke about Winston, and you better tell him before he hears it from someone else."

Maybe if I appealed to Ramsey…

"There's nothing going on with between me and Deke, though," I tried to point out.

Ramsey stopped in his tracks and I slammed up against his back. *Motherfucker.* Ramsey turned and stared down at me, and Ramsey Reed's sole attention was something to behold. But my fascination was shaken loose at his next words. "I always credited you with being a smart girl, Delaney. But you're stupid if you think there's nothing going on between you and Deke." He paused and then sighed as if he didn't want to utter his next words. But he did. "It's over for Deke, Delaney. And he'll kill Winston if you don't fix this."

Well, hell.

CHAPTER 9

Deke ~

Emotions are a funny thing.

You can go from being birds-chirping-sun-shining-happy one second to hot-white-murderous-anger the next. Now, granted, I didn't have much of a birds-chirping-sun-shining disposition, but I didn't walk around in a perpetual state of hate and anger, either.

I had been mildly irritated when Delaney had run out of class, but I knew she was pissed, so I didn't have a problem with giving her time to calm down. Fourth period had done that.

That mild irritation had morphed into annoyance though when I had seen Ramsey dragging Delaney into the eatery pavilion. For Ramsey to put his hands on a girl, there had to be a good reason, and Ramsey would never touch what was mine without cause. I should have known something was up when he texted that he'd meet us for lunch. Ramsey and Delaney sat, but I could feel the tension.

Once we were all seated to eat, that annoyance had turned into aggravation when Winston Reynolds had stormed into the pavilion and headed straight towards our table. I knew immediately that Winston approaching us had something to do with Delaney. My suspicions were confirmed when he stopped are our table, and Delaney stood up as he said, "We need to talk, Marlow."

I stood up, and that caused the entire table to stand with me. Even the girls stood up. I faced him head on. "Do we, now?" His eyes darted towards Delaney standing behind me and I almost hit him without even knowing what he was about. His eyes on Delaney were just a little too much for me.

"Winston, now's not the ti-"

I cut Delaney off. "Well, say what you have to say, Reynolds," I ordered. I knew it was going to be bad because I could feel the anxiousness radiating off Delaney, and I could even feel the tension vibrating off Ramsey from the other side of the table. He knew whatever it was that Winston Reynolds was about to tell me. My only guess for Ramsey's not telling me first was that he was giving Delaney a chance to tell me.

"I just thought you should know that…" That little hesitation showed his hand. His bravado was false, but whatever he needed to say was important enough to fake it. "…well, Delaney's mine, Deke."

'Delaney's mine.'

Those two words; two words that shouldn't be uttered by any guy but me.

Winston Reynolds approached me to tell me the Delaney belonged to him, and I knew he wouldn't be braving that unless it was the absolute truth.

You know those scenes in science class when something ices over? When the water is cracking, yet forming a bond all at the same time? That's how the blood in my veins felt right now. The cold was deep and relentless.

I want to say I might have handle this better had Delaney not jumped out from behind me and gone to stand next to Winston, but the truth was, I wouldn't have handled this well, no matter what. No matter what Delaney said, Winston's claims, what the school thought…in my head? Well, in my head, Delaney was mine the second our kiss ended, and she slapped me. And here another guy was trying to tell me she wasn't. Rage was replacing the cold rushing through my veins, and nothing good was going to come out of it.

"Deke-"

My arm snaked out, and grabbing Delaney by the nape of her neck, I forced her next to me. Ignoring Winston, and our entire audience of lunchtime students, I snarled down at her, "Align yourself with another guy like that ever again and I will fucking kill him before I make your life a living hell." I shook her body for emphasis. "Understand?" Delaney's eyes were wide and wild, but I turned my gaze back to Winston. He looked at Delaney like he wanted to save her and that just aggravated me even more.

Winston made things worse when he said, "We're engaged to be married, Deke. I…I just thought you should know that before, uh, you think of taking things further with Delaney." Murmurs ran through the pavilion like a wave.

Because I still had my hand gripping Delaney's neck, I felt her turned her body towards Winston. Now she was standing next to me facing him instead of the other way around. "What is wrong with you?!" she yelled. "I was going to tell him. You didn't have to do this, Winston. You didn't have to do this here and now!"

Delaney was engaged to marry Winston Reynolds.

"So you say," Winston countered.

"I was," she argued. "Ramsey gave me until the end of the day because I wanted to do this privately, with a chance to explain everything."

Reynolds quickly showed that he had a pair, and I was mildly impressed. "What's to explain, Delaney? You're mine. You have always been mine. Deke needs to know you're temporary if you're anything to him."

Those words again.

The corners of my vision became hazing and the next thing I knew I had my fists wrapped up in Winston's shirt, slamming him down on the table, food flying everywhere. His hands wrapped around my wrists, but that was the extent of his fight. I knew fright, and Winston Reynolds was frightened.

"Deke!" Delaney screamed. "Oh, my God! Stop it!"

I ignored Delaney because I knew Ramsey or Liam wouldn't let her get hurt. I lifted him and slammed Winston down on the table one more time for good measure. This motherfucker needed to grasp just how serious my next words were. Loud enough for the entire school to hear, I made one thing absolutely, irrevocably clear to this guy, to my friends, to the whole fucking school. "Delaney is *not* yours," I corrected. "You might have thought she was at one time, but not any longer. Delaney's *mine*. She's mine, and if you ever go near her again, I *will* fucking kill you, Reynolds."

He didn't immediately cower like a little bitch. "You don't understand. She-"

"Stay away from her!" I roared, not caring who heard. "Stay the fuck away from her. Delaney is fucking mine. *She's mine*, and..." I was at a loss. My anger was so palpable, I couldn't speak. I couldn't speak the words that would suggest Winston might have gotten to Delaney first. That rage-infused thought had me losing my shit.

I hauled Winston upright and I couldn't have stopped my right fist from forming even if I had wanted to. Delaney had asked me how did I know she was a virgin, and now faced with the knowledge that Winston Reynolds might know her in a way I believed only I would have, had me fucked-up.

My fists started raining down on Winston, and it took both Liam and Ramsey pull me off him.

Winston dropped in a bloody heap and I prayed-*prayed* Delaney wouldn't go to him. I'd kill him if she did. Then probably her.

"Deke..." Delaney whispered.

I ignored everyone around us. I ignored the phones that were out. I ignored the teachers rushing our way. I ignored my friends. I ignored everyone and everything but her. I turned towards her and I'm not sure what she saw on my face, but her eyes widened a fraction before she turned and ran.

She ran.

Delaney ran, and I ran after her, and as I ran, I heard footsteps thundering behind me. Ramsey, Liam, Emerson, and Linnie were hot on my tail. I knew Ramsey and Liam were following as accomplices, whereas the girls were running after me to make sure I didn't kill Delaney.

Because I couldn't say I wouldn't once I got my hands on her.

I'll admit this thing with her was happening rather quickly, but she's had plenty of opportunities to tell me something was going on between her and Reynolds. She could have mentioned him when I kissed her. She could have mention in all throughout second and third period. She. Could. Have.

Mentioned. Him. And even though she claimed that she was going to tell me after school today, Winston challenging me in front of everyone-in front of *her*, changed the game. There was a reason he told me now in front of everyone. I just didn't know what that reason was yet, but I would find out.

I had just rounded the corner to see Delaney slamming her locker shut, her backpack hanging off her shoulder. She was leaving. *"Delaney!"*

She froze and looked over at me. There was only twenty feet of hallway separating us, but it felt like an ocean. Her eyes went to my bloody hands and a sickness so depraved rose up inside of me. The darkness I kept hidden; the needs that made me mentally unbalanced…all of it rose to the surface.

I wanted to fuck her with her fiancé's blood all over my hands.

I wanted to watch streaks of his blood stain her body as I drove into her; his blood on her skin with her blood on my cock.

The thunderous footsteps stopped behind me and I knew everyone was frozen, waiting for my next move. And my next move was to get out of here. If I touched her…if I breathed her in, I was going to take from her things I had no right to take from her unwillingly. That's how far gone I was in my rage and sick need for her.

"Make sure she's okay," I said, my words echoing throughout the hallway, before I turned and left everyone behind me.

If I stayed, I would have ruined Delaney Martin, and I wanted her around for the long haul.

CHAPTER 10

Delaney ~

I had my feet curled up underneath my ass, hugging a pillow to my chest, wondering how everything went so wrong.

After Deke had left, I heard through gossip that Winston had to be carried to the nurse's office where they had to send him to the hospital. Deke had broken his nose and fractured a cheekbone.

I closed my eyes at the memory.

Never in a million years did I ever think that, one day, Deke Marlow would be fighting over me. It had been surreal and scary as hell. Witnessing the fact that it had taken both Ramsey and Liam to pull him off Winston was a testament to how enraged Deke had been. But what was really stupid was I somehow felt as if it had all been my fault, even though, I knew it wasn't.

None of this was my doing, I told myself for the millionth time. I'm not the one who pursued Deke. I'm not the one who kissed him. I'm not the one who dragged him to class. And I didn't feel the need to tell him about Winston because it hadn't been any of his business.

But seeing how serious Deke became at Winston's confrontation had me reevaluating a lot of my earlier beliefs. I used to think this was a bet or a game Deke was playing for entertainment value, but the image of him standing in the hallway, blood on his hands and clothes, looking like an avenging dark angel changed my mind.

That was too much emotion to be faked.

A cup of tea blocked my vision and I set the pillow down on my lap to take it. Ava held her cup in her hand as she sat next to me. Knowing Deke had left school premises, I had managed to finish the rest of my school day. Ava had spent every second she could with me, but when she hadn't been with me, Ramsey, Liam, Emerson, or Roselyn had been close by. When we were in the hallway, I had heard Deke call to them to look out for me, but I hadn't really expected them to.

"Why would Winston do that?" Ava asked. "No one in their right mind would confront anyone in that group like that." As ballsy as Ava was, even she knew better than to confront anyone in that group.

So, she wasn't wrong, and it was one of the many questions that have been plaguing me all afternoon. I took a sip of my hot tea before I said, "I don't know, Ava. It doesn't make any sense. Winston hadn't needed to do that." It still didn't make sense no matter how much I mulled over it in my head. "Even if Winston didn't think I was going to tell Deke about our arrangement, he had to know that Ramsey would have."

Ava curled her legs under her ass and mirrored my position. "Maybe he thought he could piss Deke off enough to leave you alone? Maybe Winston thought that if...I don't know, that if you were a cheater or deceitful, Deke would leave you alone."

I shook my head. "Why, though?" I asked. "Winston's been living the single life for years. He's never been interested in what I was doing. If he could sleep with other girls all these years and keep it just sex, why wouldn't he think I could do the same? Why feel threatened all of the sudden?"

Ava shrugged a shoulder. "I don't know," she replied. "Maybe because it's Deke."

I was getting a headache trying to make sense of this mess. "Who cares which boy it is? Winston never cared which girl it was."

Ava nibbled on her lower lip in thought before suggesting, "Maybe because Deke's never shown an interest in a girl before, beyond a night in bed." She set her tea down on the table and got serious. "Deke chasing after you is a big deal, Delaney. It was a big deal when he did it on Friday, and it was a big deal when he kissed you this morning, and it's a really big fucking deal that he fought over you. Deke Marlow is one of the three most influential and powerful people in this town, Delaney. His interest in you *is* a threat to your agreement with Winston. If Deke is playing for keeps, how is Winston supposed to compete with that?"

"Jesus Christ, Ava," I muttered. "It's not like we're getting married after graduation or anything. We're not even supposed to get married for another four years. And who's to say Winston doesn't meet a girl who rocks his world while he's at college? It's an agreement between two families made years ago, not the damn Ten Commandments."

"Maybe all of Winston's whoring around blinded you to the fact that this arrangement is real to him. I mean, the agreement wasn't signed in blood or anything, either one of you could change your minds now that you're adults, and your parents couldn't do anything about it."

I snorted. "Anything but not pay for our college for the next four years," I pointed out. "And I wouldn't put it past them to use that to keep the agreement binding."

"Well, I think he was trying to ruin things for you and Deke because of good ol' fashion jealousy," she replied. "Winston's been so used to you just waiting patiently in the wings, he didn't like seeing someone else interested in you. Especially, when that someone is someone like Deke Marlow." She shrugged a shoulder again. "Unfortunately for him, his plan backfired, and he got his ass kicked instead."

I groaned.

This was so above my paygrade.

I set my tea down next to Ava's on the table and ran my hands through my hair. I'd never been so confused before. I went from being a nobody to Deke Marlow's plaything, and I didn't know how to navigate my way through this.

I looked over at my friend. "I don't know what to do, Ava," I whispered. I really didn't.

Her pretty face filled with compassion and I knew my friend was worried for me. I wasn't wild like Ava. I didn't have her spunk or spirit. Ava did what Ava wanted to, and she didn't care who said what about it. "Do you like Deke, Delaney?" she asked simply.

Did I like Deke?

God, what a question.

If I was being completely honest with myself, then the answer would be, I don't know. I was curious about him. I was attracted to him. I was even attracted to him enough to know that I wouldn't put up much of a fight if he did try to sleep with me. But *like* him?

I didn't know enough about Deke to know if I liked him or not. I knew his reputation, but I didn't store anything in rumors and reputations. If I went by Ava's reputation, I'd never know the good person she could be. Rumors and reputations didn't do anything for me. I treated people how they treated me, simple as that.

"I don't know, Ava," I admitted. "I don't know him at all. I know nothing about Deke to judge if I like him or not."

Ava thought on that a bit before asking, "Do you *want* to get to know him? Do you want to like him? Sleep with him?"

That question was much easier to answer. "Yeah, if…if I could get past all the crazy inside him, maybe."

Ava grinned. "Oh, Delaney," she chuckled. "Crazy is the sexiest part of a man."

My eyes almost bugged out. "I'd have to disagree, Ava. Did you see what he did to Winston?"

She cocked her head sideways and regarded me silently before asking another candid question. "I'm going to ask you something and I want you to answer me honestly," she started out. "When Ramsey and Liam pulled him off Winston and he was standing there like a raging god, bloody and wild out of his mind, did that turn you on?"

I could feel the heat crawl up my chest, over my neck, and throughout my face. I had still been in shock at the turn of events when Ramsey and Liam had pulled Deke off Winston, but when Deke had turned to face me, the look on his face had been pure uncontrollable fury. He looked like a dark storm. I had run from him out of fear for my safety, but when we had faced off in the hallway, and he stood there with blood on his hands and clothing, looking as he was one movement away from killing someone, I *had* been turned on.

I had been turned on in a wicked, unnatural way. In that moment I would have let Deke Marlow do whatever he wanted to me.

Winston had be the catalyst that turned Deke's toying and teasing into a battle of wills. The switch had been flipped and the Deke Marlow that was staring me down in the hallway after the fight was the *real* Deke Marlow. I suspected his friends knew it too, and that's why they had followed. They wanted to make sure he didn't kill me.

I wasn't going to lie to Ava when I was asking for her advice and help. "Yes," I confessed.

I thought she'd get giddy or sly, maybe joke about it. But, instead, she looked sorry for me. Like she knew I was going swimming with the sharks with my leg bleeding and no one would be able to save me. "You guys are probably going to crash and burn, you know that, right?"

"I'm terrified, Ava," I admitted, "but not enough to stop this." She nodded her head sadly. "This morning when I slapped him, I meant that. I wanted nothing to do with him, but now...now, I don't know how not to want him."

"That's because he's done the one thing no one has ever done for you, Delaney," she replied. "He fought for you. He made you feel like you matter, and that's a dangerous drug for girls like us."

Again, she wasn't wrong.

CHAPTER 11

Deke ~

The bag swung back and forth, but it still didn't feel as if I was hitting it hard enough. It didn't matter that my hands were all busted up from Reynold's face, either. I welcomed the sting and the burn. Hell, I wanted to kick his ass all over again.

After I left school, I texted the gang to let them know I was fine, and just needed a breather. And after that, I had gone straight home and to our home gym. Well, my home gym. My parents were never home, and when they were, they sure as hell weren't working out in here.

I was still feeling unhinged, and rage was still coursing through my blood. I needed an outlet before I killed Winston or attacked Delaney, because, *Christ*, that need was still simmering underneath the surface of my moral line. Not killing Winston. Nope. I was perfectly fine with that.

The need to attack Delaney; that dark, visceral need was still with me and I wouldn't go anywhere near her until I got it under control.

I had every intention on commanding her body and ruling her pleasure. I had every intention of taking her brutally; virgin or not. I had every intention of destroying her.

But she had to be willing.

That was not negotiable. I might want to dance on the line of moral propriety with her, but I didn't want to cross over into immoral responsibility. And the way I was feeling now, I'd take her just to prove she belonged to me and not Winston, and that's not how I wanted us to get down. I wanted no one else in that bedroom with us, figuratively or literally.

When Delaney and I finally do come together, it's going to be because she wants it-she wants *me*. But before that happens, she'll know and understand that, after she gives me full consent to own her body, she will never be able to take it back. She'll have to know that, and dissect what that means, before I get her under me. I planned on taking her farther than I've ever taken anyone else. I planned on letting her see the monster, and I could only pray that she'll stay afterwards.

The ringing of my phone cut through the music blasting through the gym, and I knew I had to answer it or else it'd never stop ringing.

I turned from the punching bag and walked towards the speaker system that commanded the surround sound. Turning it off, I grabbed my phone from the wall table and swiped to answer. "What?"

"Seriously, Deke?" my father replied. "A fight?"

I rolled my eyes even though he couldn't see me. My breaths were deep and rapid from my workout, but that didn't stop me from letting out a huff. "Since when do you give a fuck if I get in a fight or not?" This was probably the tenth conversation I've had with my father since I hit my teen years; I wasn't confused about whether the man gave a shit about me or not. He let my mother deal with me, if needed, and her form of concern and affection was usually a massive deposit into my bank account.

"Since you're now a senior in high school and you'll be going out into the real world soon," he barked. "Real men don't get into fistfights to solve their issues, Deke."

"No," I agreed. "They just bribe other men to look the other way."

"Watch how you talk to me, son," he hissed. "I'm your father and I'm the one who makes your lifestyle possible. Don't forget that."

What my father failed to realize was that I was very aware of the fact that he needed me more than I needed him. Thanks to Ramsey's foresight, me, Ram, and Liam didn't need any of our parents at this stage of the game. "Fine," I dared. "Cut me off and kick me out. I don't give a fuck, Dad."

There was a couple of seconds of silence, and I knew he knew who won this round. "Over a girl, Deke?" he said, ignoring my dare. "Why on earth would you get into a fight over a fucking girl when there are millions of them available to you?"

"How do you even know I got into a fight?" Lord knows I didn't update him with what went on in my life.

"The school called because they had to," he informed me. "Apparently, the other boy had to be taken to the hospital because you broke his nose and fractured one of his cheekbones."

I snorted. "So, that's why you called? Because you need confirmation on how bad it was in case his family sues?" The phone call made sense now.

"No," he barked into the phone again. "I called to tell you to get your shit together. People don't solve their issues with their fists in the real world, Deke. I am not going to have you destroy everything I've built because you can't keep a civil head."

"You mean everything your grandfather built," I reminded him. "You may have brought more to the table during your reign, Dad, but that table was already there when you sat down to dinner."

"You're missing the point, Deke!"

I couldn't stop the growl that emitted from my soul. For eighteen years this man has done nothing to raise me, and he thinks he can call me now and play the role of father...*fuck, too*. "I sent that boy to the hospital because he had the balls to come to me and tell me my girl belonged to him, Dad," I snapped. "He's lucky he's not dead!"

"It's just pussy, Deke!" my father roared over the phone. "Let him have the bitch and pick a girl who doesn't need to be fucked by a bunch of different guys!"

Had my father been standing in front of me while saying that, I would have killed him.

I took a deep breath, and counted to five, before clearing things up for my dad. "Listen to me, Dad, and listen well. I don't give a flying fuck what you say or threaten. I am not giving up this girl for anyone, least of all you. And if you ever talk about her like that again, you'll regret it."

"I will not have you fucking everything up for a girl, Deke," he repeated.

"I'm not," I replied. "But, even if I were, I don't answer to you, Dad." And I didn't. At this point in my life, I had more respect for the people who really raised me and took care of me. I'd listen to the maid, gardener, housekeeper, and cook before I'd listen to either of my fucked-up parents.

"Watch it, Deke," he threatened again.

I smirked. "*You* watch it, Dad," I threw back. "You keep sticking your nose where it doesn't belong, I'll be sending out an announcement introducing you to your new pregnant daughter-in-law by the end of the week. *Do. Not. Fuck. With. Me.*"

My quick reminder that I was now, legally, an adult shot down his bravado. "Just...stay out of trouble, Deke," he grumbled. "You think you can manage that?"

I rolled my eyes again. "I'll see what I can do," I deadpanned before hanging up on him.

I wasn't a fucking idiot. I knew grown folks shouldn't solve their issues with their fists. However, I also knew the justice system was super corrupt. I just happened to be one of the fortunate people who could buy my way out of trouble. Everyone had a price; some were just higher than others. And if someone couldn't be bought, well, they could be threatened or blackmailed. If I couldn't buy my way out of trouble, I knew Ramsey would have no problem helping me blackmail my way out of it. That was Ramsey's specialty. He knew the dirtiest dirt on the entire town of Sands Cove and almost everyone who has ever done business with his father. I didn't fear landing in jail because between me, Ram, and Liam, there wasn't anything we couldn't get out of.

My phone rang in my hand, and I answered it willingly this time. "What's up?"

"Just making sure you're not off pillaging an innocent village somewhere," Liam joked.

I smiled for the first time since lunch at school. "Nope," I answered. "I'm at home working out in the gym." I grabbed the bottle of water and took a swig before asking, "How is she?"

"Traumatized, I think," he huffed out. "Seriously, though, she seemed…quiet."

"Christ, Lee, she was already a quiet wallflower," I pointed out, "how much more quiet could she have been?"

He let out a deep sigh. "She looked sad, man," he finally admitted.

I ignored the pang in my chest and told him, "Sampson called to scold me about the fight."

Liam laughed. "Are you serious?" I went on to recite the conversation, and by the time I was finished, Liam was cracking up. "What a fucking fool."

"I should get Delaney pregnant," I said seriously. "It'd solve all my problems if I did."

Liam's laugh dwindled to a chuckle. "I wish my moral compass was pure enough to tell you that getting Delaney pregnant at 18-years-old is a bad idea, but it's not, and I can't. If Roz told me tomorrow she was pregnant, I'd be ecstatic as hell."

"Linnie would be an awesome mom," I laughed, encouraging Liam's madness.

"So, if I knock her up, I can blame you?" he asked, a smile in his voice.

"Sure," I quipped. "Just let me and Ram know so we can get to work. There's no way our children aren't going to grow up together."

Liam's laugh was cut short with a real solid thought. "Christ, Deke," he breathed. "Ramsey's already out of his mind when it comes to Emerson. Could you imagine his level of insanity if he got her pregnant?"

I laughed. "I got a hundred that she'd kill him before the second trimester."

Liam laughed. "I got a grand that says before the first month is up."

CHAPTER 12

Delaney ~

It was Wednesday afternoon and Deke was absent again. He hadn't shown up for school yesterday and I hadn't seen him this morning either. I hadn't seen him in second period, and when he was still missing during third period, I knew he wasn't at school again. Winston was a no show also, but that was to be expected.

I also couldn't deny the pang in my chest at Deke's sudden silence. In addition to him not being at school, he hasn't called or texted or anything. When third period started without him, I had finally been forced to accept the effect he now had on my life. It was strange to know that it's only been a few days since that party, but in these few short days, Deke's impacted my life in a way I never thought anyone could.

Instead of doing homework last night, I had spent the entire evening reevaluating my current state in life. When mine and Winston's parents as arranged our marriage at the age of ten, I hadn't a clue what it had meant. Winston had been my friend, and at 10-years-old, the idea of spending forever with my friend sounded just fine to me.

As the years passed, I began to realize my personality was more solitary than outgoing, and I used our arrangement as a crutch to not have to get to know anyone beyond superficial acknowledgement. Ava had come into my life when we were both thirteen, and she hadn't let me be shy with her. She had fascinated me with her loud personality and ballsy attitude. I'd never been anyone's pushover, but I wasn't sparkly like Ava. I cared what people thought of me. I cared if I did well in school. I cared if I was kind to people. I cared, period.

Earlier this year, when Ramsey had gone balls out and tried to humiliate Emerson in front of the entire school, I remember feeling sick for her. But then I remember how everyone had been struck speechless when she had walked out of Windsor without a backward glance with her head held high. I

47

remember feeling envy at that kind of strength. Because, let me tell you, there is an impenetrable strength in not giving a shit what other people thought of you. It set you free in a way that nothing else could.

Even when she had returned and Ramsey had dropped to his knees for her in front of everyone, he hadn't given a shit what anyone thought. His only thought was that of Emerson and her forgiveness, and I had been one of the girly-girls who had cried and clapped when she forgave him.

I saw it again when Liam had lost his mind over Roselyn. He fell in love with her and he hadn't cared who knew or what his pursuit of her made him look like. When the rumors had started flying about Roselyn dating both Liam and Deke, he had shut that shit down like a tsunami taking out a small village. No one really knew if she dated both of them or not but, even if she had, no one would say a word. Besides, if anyone did, it would be because they were jealous. I might be a virgin, but even I knew being bedded by both Liam and Deke at the same time would be an experience most girls would kill for.

The other reason no one could pinpoint if the rumors were true or not was because if you look at all of them, Deke and Roselyn showed no signs of anything other than friendship. And Liam and Deke were as close as they ever were. There wasn't a hint of jealousy or awkwardness anywhere amongst them.

"I feel like it's the calm before the storm," Ava mumbled as she leaned against the locker next to mine. We had just left fourth period and were putting our stuff away before heading to lunch.

I opened my locker and stuffed my backpack inside. "I know," I agreed. "It's like…I feel like I'm trapped waiting for…something. I don't know…"

Ava hugged her books to her chest. "You do know that you're going to have to make a decision about Winston when Deke does finally come back to school, right?"

I knew she was right. I let this arrangement go on for so long because I had been fine with it. I had been fine with marrying a man I got along with because I've never been a passionate person. I didn't need a love of a lifetime. I was used to my parents' marriage, and that marriage lacked love like ninety percent of Sands Cove's marriages. But Deke inspired that passion, and I wasn't going to pretend like he didn't any longer.

"I think-"

"Delaney?" I whipped around at the sound of my name, and I saw Emerson Andrews and Roselyn Bell walking towards me.

What. The. Hell?

I shut my locker closed and glanced at Ava. She looked wary but that could be for any number of reasons. It wasn't a secret that she's slept with both Liam and Ramsey at one point in her life. I could see how Emerson and Roselyn approaching us might make things awkward.

I waited until both girls were standing in front of us before saying, "Hey, Emerson. Roselyn." They were such pretty girls, it was hard not to be intimidated a bit. Emerson had gorgeous brown hair with hypnotic grey eyes and a body built like a woman's, whereas, Roselyn was dainty with rainbow-colored hair, big blue eyes, and a tiny nose ring.

Roselyn smiled, while Emerson's eyes darted towards Ava, and I was immediately flooded with anxiety. Ava wasn't weak, and she wasn't the type to back down, but even after all these months, Emerson was still an unknown. She came to Sands Cove because her father had killed her mother and her aunt had taken her in because, at the time, she had still been a minor. But nowadays, she lived with Ramsey. The thing was, any girl brave, strong, or crazy enough to go up against Ramsey Reed had to be packing a powerful punch.

Emerson Andrews was a goddamn legend.

Emerson's eyes bounced back and forth between me and Ava before finally settling on Ava. "Can I be frank about something?" Ava and I just nodded silently. "I don't care that you've slept with Ramsey, Ava," she said, shocking the shit out of both of us. "If I worried about every girl Ramsey's ever slept with, I wouldn't be able to live in this town, much less go to this school. I don't care what he did before I came along, I really don't." She shrugged a shoulder. "Besides, it'd be an insult to Ramsey if I let the girls he's slept with bother me. It would mean I didn't believe the things he tells me, and that's just not the case. I know Ramsey loves me. I know he'd give his life for me. And I definitely know he'd never cheat on me. It doesn't bother me, Ava, if it doesn't bother you."

I glanced over at Roselyn and she threw her hands up in a surrender motion. "Don't look at me," she laughed. "I'm the last person to judge anyone on their past and the shit they've done." She put her hands down and smiled. "I'm with Emer on this. The last thing I'm worried about is Liam's past."

I looked over at Ava since this wasn't my conversation and she looked…humbled. "I…I know I…I know what my reputation is," she stated. "And I've earned most of what anyone has ever said about me, but whatever anyone has ever heard of me, they've never heard that I sleep with guys who are taken, because I don't." It was hard for me not to get teary-eyed at Ava owning her shit. She was such an awesome person underneath her actions, and I hated how so many people would never know that. "Ramsey and Liam were so long ago, I honestly haven't given them so much as a thought in years."

Emerson smiled, and it felt like a stamp of approval. "Well, I felt like we needed to clear that up since you're Delaney's best friend and she belongs to Deke now."

She said it so casually factual it took a second for the words to register. "Whoa, what?"

Roselyn's smile joined with Emerson's. "Look, Delaney, I know Deke can be rather…much, but you're a smart girl. After what happened Monday, you have to know that Deke's claim on you is solid."

"Why, though?" I asked. "In all the years I've known who Deke's been, he's never paid me any mind. Now, all of a sudden, he's interested, and I'm just supposed to accept that? Rearrange my life with no explanation, whatsoever?"

"I don't think you have a choice, Delaney," Emerson answered. "Deke's not going to let you go."

I shook my head. "I don't understand any of this," I admitted.

Roselyn snorted. "Who does? This is Deke Marlow we're talking about. Hell, trying to figure him, Liam, or Ramsey out is like trying to understand what makes the Bermuda Triangle tick. Give up the ghost, girl, and just go with it. Trust me. You'll have fewer headaches that way."

I ignored their advice and asked the one question I'd been dying to. "Why's he not in school?"

Emerson's eyes darted towards Roselyn's before returning those grey eyes back on me. "The truth?" she asked.

"Yes, please." Roselyn started gnawing on her lower lip, and she gave me the same sad look Ava had when I had told her I was attracted to Deke. She looked like she felt sorry for me.

Emerson cleared her throat and told me the truth. "He's staying away because he's in such a bad headspace, he's afraid for your safety."

All the air left my lungs at her statement. "What...what do you mean?"

Roselyn let out a deep sigh. "The boys are really hush, hush when it comes to...their man-bonding, but whatever it is you did to get on Deke's radar...well, it's serious for him. That's all I know."

I looked over at Emerson and asked, "What has Ramsey told you?" I knew she'd never breach his confidence, but I still had to ask.

She looked sad for me too. "Nothing. Roselyn's right about their bond. But I can tell you that there's no outrunning Deke Marlow, Delaney. You're pretty much fucked, chic."

CHAPTER 13

Deke ~

I still wasn't sure if it was a good idea to come back to school, but I couldn't stay away any longer. For years, I hadn't paid any attention to Delaney Martin, and in a matter of one Friday night, she was all I could think about now.

I knew from the gang's reports that Delaney was keeping to herself, but that didn't surprise me; she always did. While she chitchatted with people here and there, Ava was her only real friend. What had surprised me was the phone call I got from Emerson telling me all about the talk she and Linnie had had with Delaney and Ava, and it made me fall in love with my two girls that much more. The fact that Emerson and Roselyn would clear the air with Ava, just to make her and Delaney more comfortable about my pursuit, showed me what real class acts those two girls were. While Ramsey and Liam knew the extent of my obsession with Delaney, I hadn't shared the details with the girls, and they still went to bat for me.

As per usual, I was hanging out in front of school waiting for the bell to ring and for Delaney to pass by. I wasn't exactly sure how all this was going to go down, but during my self-imposed hiatus, I realized I needed to get the full story on her and Reynolds. I also needed to know if she's slept with him. Now, with my past, I'm the last person to judge, but I wanted to know because I needed to know if he had a hold on her or not. Most girls were funny about the guy they give their virginity to, and I needed to find out exactly what all Reynolds meant to Delaney. I already knew their families were close if they had arranged a goddamn marriage at the age of fucking ten, so I already had that working against me. I needed to know how Delaney felt about the asshole. I had no doubt I'd have Delaney in the end, but I wanted to know what I was up against.

I felt the charge in the air a split second before I saw Delaney and Ava walking together towards the front doors of the school. I didn't bother with

51

goodbyes as I knew the crew already knew where I was with this. I hustled my way over to the girls, ignored Ava, grabbed Delaney by the arm and dragged her around the back of the building, and the most important fact in all this?

She let me.

I pinned her up against the building and caged her in with my palms flat on either side of her. She adjusted her backpack over her shoulder as she looked up at me putting on a brave face. My eyes darted over to her scar, and just like that, my dick was hard.

"You're here," she muttered quietly, and my entire body stilled with the implication of her words. *Delany fucking missed me.* Or, at the very least, she wondered about me.

My hand came off the building, landed on her shoulder, and slid across her collarbone, down over her left tit, and kept going until it stopped at her hip. Delaney's breath hitched as I slid my hand upwards underneath her uniform shirt and wrapped it around the flank of her waist.

Nothing ever felt so good as my hand on Delaney Martin's bare flesh.

I leaned down until my lips grazed her ear. "Did you miss me?"

"Deke…" she moaned, and I lost all common sense.

I pushed up against her, so she was completely blocked off by my body, and not waiting for permission, I slid my hand down the front of her uniform pants causing the button to pop off and the zipper to bust open. Delaney's backpack slid off her shoulder, and her hands fisted in my shirt, as her head dropped to rest on my chest. She wasn't stopping me and that shamed her to the point where she couldn't look at me, but I was okay with that. We'd work on that later.

I slid my hand in between her legs, and the second my fingers touched her wet flesh, I knew whatever she had with Reynolds didn't matter. Her grip threatened to tear the fabric of my shirt as I slid my fingers back and forth between her pussy lips. It sounded like she might be crying, but I wasn't sure, and I wasn't going to stop to find out. As long as she wasn't telling me to stop or pushing me away, nothing was going to stop me from making Delaney cum like this.

When I felt my fingers were lubed up enough from her wetness, I slid one into her pussy, and it was so tight, there's no way she wasn't a virgin. Delaney threw her head back hard enough I could hear its impact against the building. Her eyes were screwed shut, but I could see the wetness decorating her lashes.

Yep, she'd been crying.

I leaned in and did the one thing I've been wanting to do since I cornered her at that party last Friday. I had my fingers buried deep in her pussy, going in and out, as I licked that fucking scar on her face. Delaney whimpered, and I wasn't sure how I was going to get out of this without fucking her right here in front of whoever might happen by.

I pulled back to look at her. "Have you fucked Reynolds?" I growled. "Has he ever touched you, Lamb?" Her eyes shot open, and she looked breathtaking in tears. "Or are my fingers the first fingers to ever touch this pussy?" Delaney nodded, and because she looked positively torn up about her admission, I knew she had nodded to my fingers being the first to ever touch her. "You're going to explain about Reynolds, but I need you to know that, no matter what, you're mine, Delaney. You. Are. Mine."

Her eyes shut again when I started upping the tempo of my fingers. I was finger fucking Delaney hard and deep, and I didn't care that we were out in the open at school. I was doing my best to shield her with my body, but it wouldn't be too difficult to deduce what we were doing.

My name was a heartbreaking sob on her lips, "Deke..."

"It's okay, Delaney," I breathed against her face; against her scar. "Cum on my fingers, baby. I got you. I *promise* I got you." Her nails dug into my skin through the fabric of my shirt and she let out the throatiest moan as she came all over my hand.

We stood there in complete silence as Delaney started coming off her high. My hand was still down her pants, but I knew it wouldn't be long before the reality of what she just let me do set in and she lost her shit. I wasn't confused. Delaney wanted me, but she didn't *want* to want me.

When her eyes opened and latched onto mine, I pulled my fingers out of her pants, stuck them in my mouth, and licked them clean. Her eyes widened and I could actually see the panic start to take hold in those beautiful eyes of hers. Delaney had lost herself to me and it was written all over her face, plain as day, how humiliated she was over the fact.

"De...Deke...oh, God," she muttered as her hand flew to her pants and her face rushed red when she realized the zipper and button of her pants were useless. "Oh, shit. Oh, shit," she rambled on.

"Delaney-"

Her hands pushed at my chest and I knew our moment was over. She was going to go back to not wanting to want me. "I can't believe I let you do that," she hissed. "I can't believe...I...what the hell was I thinking letting you...*oh, Christ.*"

"Delaney-"

Her eyes were blazing, and she was nothing but a ball of unchartered emotions. "I don't even *like* you, Deke," she claimed.

Now I was getting pissed. I was willing to grant her some confusion and embarrassment because Delaney Martin was not the kind of girl who let guys finger fuck her in public, but I knew she liked me. She just didn't *want* to like me. "Your scent on my fingers contradicts that statement, Lamb," I bit out. "Or do you let all the guys you don't like finger your pussy like a-"

"Fuck you, Deke Marlow!" she yelled in my face. "I'm not...I don't..."

I grabbed her by her shoulders and held her firm against the wall. "I know you're pissed that you caved when you don't want to like me, Delaney," I allowed. "But you are not going to act like what just happened wasn't always *going* to happen. You missed me these past two days. Own it and quit being a little bitch about it."

Her spine straightened, and I knew I was pulling out the Delaney no one ever saw; the Delaney Martin no one knew. "I'll show you a bitch, Deke Marlow," she threatened, her voice still and absolute.

I cupped her face in my hands and welcomed her threat. "I hope you do, Lamb," I said. "I hope to fuck you do, because the second you start showing me what you're capable of, I can start showing you what *I'm* capable of." Her breathing hitched, and my dick reminded me that he was still hard from the finger fucking. "You think you've seen me at my worst because Reynolds has a broken nose and fucked-up face? Baby, that's nothing compared to what my conscience allows me to do and still sleep at night." I leaned in and whispered against her ear, "Show me how much of a bitch you can be, Delaney. Show me, so I can ruin you. Show me, so I can't fuck you up so badly, your mind cracks along with your heart and soul, baby."

I pulled back so she could look into my face; into my eyes and see just how serious I was. I wanted to ruin Delaney. I wanted to break her into a million fucking pieces until I was the only one who could put her back together. Delaney called to the darkest parts of me and I knew I'd never let her go.

"I'm not weak," she whispered.

I let go of her face and took a step back. "Maybe not," I allowed. "But if you're going to fight this-*us*, well, you should know what you're going up against, Delaney."

"And what's that?"

"I'm Deke Marlow," I stated simply. "You go up against me, you go up against Ramsey, Liam, Emerson, and Roselyn, baby. So, tell me how strong your inner bitch is now?"

CHAPTER 14

Delaney ~

Deke was right.

He was right, and I knew it. I'd always known it.

Deke was a package deal. Even if they all went to separate colleges, nothing would break the bond Deke had with Ramsey, Liam, and the girls. It was obvious in how they had hung around in the shadows these past couple of days watching out for me while he'd been gone. It was obvious in how Emerson and Roselyn had made the effort to make Ava feel comfortable around them all. They would back Deke's play no matter how it ended up.

They'd bury my body if Deke needed that from them.

And now we were sitting in Deke's car, missing first period, because he lured me to his car with the promise of a safety pin for my uniform pants. But if I'm being completely honest with myself, I needed these few precious moments. Letting him do what he did still had me a little flustered.

Even with my admission to Ava last night about being attracted to Deke, I hadn't been expecting to feel such a substantial amount of weight to be lifted from my chest when I saw he was back. Deke shouldn't have been able to affect me so strongly after one confrontation on Friday, and one day of bullshit on Monday.

I had told Ava I was attracted to him, but I was starting to fear it was more than mere attraction. I let Deke bring me to orgasm without a care to my reputation or my arrangement with Winston, which, let's face it, was coming to an end. And, while I never judged Ava for being wild, having experienced my first orgasm at the hands of a hot guy, well…let's just say, I understood a lot better now how a girl could get carried away. I also wouldn't judge Roselyn if the rumors about her were true. Deke had me seeing Jesus, and I couldn't imagine an experience where Liam McCellan joined in.

Holy shit.

Deke was turned in his seat looking at me, holding the safety pin hostage, as he demanded, "Now, tell me about Reynolds."

I rolled my eyes but told him, anyway. "When we were ten, our parents had sat us down and told us we were going to marry each other." I shrugged a shoulder. "At that age, I hadn't really understood the implications of what they were saying, but Winston was my friend. It hadn't seemed like a bad idea to marry my friend. Over the years, we were kind of brainwashed into accepting that our getting married made sense. Lots of families with money or dynasties get married to secure business relationships or acquire more wealth. Winston and I bought into it and, quite frankly, it saved me from having to…I don't know. Knowing my future was with Winston, I didn't have to meet boys or go on dates. The arrangement worked for me because…well, in case you haven't noticed it all these years, I'm a pretty private person."

"And all of Reynolds' fucking around?" he asked.

"I didn't care," I answered truthfully.

"How could you not care if your future husband was sleeping with the entire town of Sands Cove?" Deke's face was impassive as he asked his questions, but like I said, Deke had a hell of a poker face.

I let out a sigh, already tired of this conversation. "Because I don't care about him like that."

"You don't care about him like that?" he repeated.

"No." A part of me wanted, so badly, to tell Deke this was none of his business, but I didn't want to be a hypocrite. I just let this guy do something to me that I've never let anyone else do. That was proof enough that Deke's hold on me was stronger than I wanted it to be. "We tried being…uh, romantic back when we were like fourteen, and, well, I don't know about him, but I felt nothing."

Deke's hand latched around my upper arm in a painful grip. "What do you mean, *romantic?*"

"We kissed," I yelped. "We just kissed, you goddamn lunatic!" He immediately let go of my arm and gestured for me to continue. *Jesus.* "We kissed, and I didn't feel anything. When it was clear that we'd never have a passionate marriage, Winston started looking to other girls for his kicks, and I just went about my business."

Deke's eyes were like liquid emeralds when he asked, "And just now? When I had my fingers in your pussy? Did you feel something then?"

I tried not to squirm in my seat, but I couldn't help it. His words reminded me of just how sensitive I was down there. "You know I did," I hissed. I knew I needed to come to terms with my surrender, but Deke's arrogance and high-handed ways made that hard. I was attracted to him, but he made it hard to like him when he was being a dick.

He didn't say anything for a few torturous seconds, before he reached across the console of his car, and fastened the safety pin to my pants. "This should hold you until you get a new pair of pants from the office," he said casually as if this morning hasn't been full of 'what the fucks'.

"Deke-"

His green eyes snapped to mine, and I could feel my willpower dwindling down more than it already had. My leg was bleeding, and I was diving into the ocean, exactly where the sharks lurked. "I'm going to give you today to…come to terms with this thing between us, Delaney," he said. "I will give you the rest of the day to…get your mind together. But after tonight, you're mine. Understand?" I nodded because I didn't know what else to do. "I'm coming for you tomorrow, Lamb." I could feel my breath leave me as he got out of his car, walked around, and opened my door to help me out.

And I let him. I let him, because I wasn't sure what came next.

Deke grabbed my hand and started pulling me behind him when I yanked my arm back, bringing him to a halt. He turned and looked down at me, his looks and commanding presence screwing with my head and heart. "What does that mean, exactly?"

Instead of answering me, Deke's hands slid up my face until they were tangled in my hair and he had my back up against his car. His lips came crashing down on mine and all I could do was grab his arms and hold on for dear life.

This kiss was powerful and consuming. His tongue was doing more than just invading my mouth; it was invading my soul. Deke was kissing me as if he was told he'd never be able to kiss a girl ever again. His hold in my hair was absolute, and so tight, my scalp started to hurt. He had his body pressed so closely to mine that I could feel his erection digging into my stomach.

I never knew you could put so much feeling into a single kiss. I never knew you could lose your mind with just a kiss. I never viewed kissing as foreplay. What Deke had done to me earlier, that's what I always considered foreplay.

But a kiss? A simple kiss?

Granted, there was nothing simple about Deke Marlow, but all I knew was that I wanted this kiss to go on forever. I wanted this passion to go on forever. I always wondered how Emerson and Roselyn didn't suffocate under the constant dominant personalities of Ramsey and Liam, but if their obsessions made those girls feel even a fraction of what Deke was making me feel right now…well, I understood a little better now. Ava had been right when she said having a guy fight for you and make you matter was dangerous for girls like us; girls who were neglected and unloved.

Deke finally broke away from me, but his breathing was labored every bit as mine was. His green eyes held me captive as he said, *"That's* what it means, Delaney." It took me a second to remember the question I had even asked him. "It means, tomorrow night, I'm coming for you and we're going to spend the entire weekend together."

I knew the answer even before I asked it, but I needed to hear him say the words. I wanted there to be no confusion. "Doing what?"

His thumb brushed my lower lip. "What do you think?" he replied. "I'm going to spend all weekend taking everything you have, Lamb. I'm going to spend all weekend fucking you so raw and relentlessly, you're going to hate me by the time I'm done with you."

My entire body broke out in shivers. His words were not the romantic words every girl dreams of. They were promises of future nightmares. "How you do you know I don't already hate you?"

"Because if you did, I wouldn't have your scent on my fingers or your flavor on my tongue," he snarled, reminding me of how he licked his fingers off after bringing me to orgasm. "You're a good girl, Delaney. You've always been a good girl. You're a quiet, smart, beautiful little wallflower," he whispered. "If you hated me, you would never have let me finger your pussy in public just now. You're not that way."

"That doesn't mean I don't hate you," I replied. "Lots of people have hate-sex."

Then Deke did something I hadn't anticipated. His hands fisted tighter in my hair and he had my head pulled back so far, my back bowed. He leaned down, and before I knew what he was about, Deke latched onto my neck and the bite was swift, brutal and bloody. He broke my flesh open, and I cried out in pain. He sucked and tore at my flesh and the pain was horrible. *"Deke!"*

His head shot up and I could see my blood on his lips. My knees threatened to buckle because the sight was overwhelming and obscene. I watched as he licked his lips and said, "I hope you do hate me, Delaney. That way my conscience won't be bothered by all the things I'm going to do to you."

He had a conscience?

CHAPTER 15

Deke ~

We were all gathered in Ramsey's father's study, but I suppose it was more Ramsey's study than his father's. I mean, a person had to actually *live* in the house to utilize any of the rooms. I was sitting on a barstool, while Liam and Roselyn took up the left side of the couch, and Ramsey was leaning his ass up against the desk with Emerson sitting on the desk next to him.

"We only have three more months before school out," Liam pointed out. "We gotta figure this shit out, and soon. My dad's calling me more and more these days, and I don't want to tell him to go get fucked without a plan in place."

"Well, we're all expected to go to college," Ramsey reminded us. "The only problem is the girls." Emerson let out a soft snort, and I had to smile. She loved Ramsey, but she didn't seem to suffer from the same insanity he did when it came to their relationship. I believed in my heart that Emerson could walk away from Ramsey and still be capable of functioning in life; Ramsey couldn't.

"You guys are supposed to go to Blaineview, right?" Roselyn asked. "You all three have been pre-selected and registered, right?" She shrugged a shoulder. "You guys can still go to Blaineview, while Em and I go to Columbia."

As sexist as it sounded, all the guys and very few girls were expected to all go to Blaineview University. It was partnered with Windsor Academy and knew what it took to continue to groom us into being little robotic heirs. Most of the girls at Windsor were allowed to apply and go to whatever college they wanted because, generally, the sons of Sands Cove were the ones who took over the family empires. There are a few rare incidences where the girls took over, but it really depended on the family's business. Oh, we were allowed to apply at whatever other colleges we wanted to also, but we were expected to go to Blaineview.

Ramsey side-eyed Linnie. "You're out of your mind if you think I'll be at Blaineview while Emerson is at Columbia, Roselyn."

I glanced over at Emerson and hid a smile as she rolled her eyes at Ramsey's statement. Once upon a time, Ramsey's comment would have kicked off a full-blown war between the two, but these days, Emerson had Ramsey by the balls, and we all knew it. *He* knew it.

But before she could remark on Ramsey's comments, Liam spoke up. "Yeah, Roz," he started, "no way are you and Emerson going to be clear across the country. That's not happening, baby."

"So, what?" Emerson asked, finally speaking up. "You guys just hand over your black credit cards until Roselyn and I are drowning in mimosas, diamonds, and charity events?" *Damn, the girl had spunk.* "No, thank you. I need my education," she huffed. "How else am I expected to support myself when I finally kill Ramsey and he's unable to bring home a paycheck any longer?"

Liam and Roselyn laughed, and I smiled, but the girl wasn't far off. As much as they loved each other, if I got a call in the middle of the night saying Emerson had killed Ramsey in a fit of rage, I wouldn't be surprised; vice versa.

Emerson looked over at me. "And what about Delaney?" she asked. "That girl is smarter than a whip, and you're crazy if you don't think she wants to go to college, Deke."

My back straightened because I knew she was right. I had no doubt Delaney's been accepted into a number of colleges because she's spent her entire life focusing on school, and I knew her grades were damn near perfect. But that didn't take away from how things were going to turn out for her.

"I mean, she has a point, Deke," Linnie chimed in. "Emerson and I might be open to a compromise, but what about Delaney?"

Ramsey snorted. "Compromise, my fucking ass," he rumbled. "If we decide to go to Blaineview, instead of just starting a business now, Emerson's going to go with me. End of fucking story."

"I can't go to Blaineview, Ramsey," Emerson argued. "I never applied, and even if I had, I don't have the family legacy to get in."

We all watched as Ramsey reached out, grabbed Emerson by her arm, yanking her off the desk, and pulled her to stand in between his spread legs. "The second we clear that goddamn graduation podium in a couple of months, you're going to be my *wife*, Emerson," he hissed. "That's all the fucking family legacy you need to get into Blaineview."

The room was silent, but I didn't miss the small head nod she gave Ramsey as she placed a hand on his chest to calm him down. I felt for the guy, though. Roselyn brining up Delaney had reminded me that what I felt for Delaney probably wasn't even close to what Ramsey felt for Emerson.

"Okay," Liam piped up, breaking the tense moment, "how about we see what we can do to get the girls into Blain-"

"What if I don't want to go to Blaineview, Liam?" Roselyn challenged.

"Sweet Baby Jesus," he breathed out, before channeling his inner Ramsey. "I don't really give a fuck, Roz. You were never going to go to Columbia or wherever the fuck else you applied, anyway."

Linnie gasped. "What does that mean?" Liam shot a glance at Ramsey, and I folded my arms across my chest, and got comfortable, waiting for the upcoming fireworks.

"Goddamn it," Ramsey growled as Emerson stepped back and started looking back and forth between him and Liam.

"What's going on?" she asked.

Ramsey moved his head side to side, cracking his neck, before he said, "We were hoping you girls would be so madly in love with us that you'd follow us anywhere, therefore, letting you guys decide your own futures, but *noooooooooooo*...you guys had to go and be difficult."

Roselyn jumped up off the couch. "Meaning?" she asked, hands planted on her hips.

Liam stood up also and I laughed as he gave up the fight. "You two she-devils are registered to attend Blaineview with us. Ramsey and I set it up a few weeks ago. We were just hoping you'd want to go *willingly*."

Emerson let out a soft, defeated laugh. "You're such a manipulating bastard, Ramsey," she said shaking her head.

Ramsey eyed her and simply said, "I know. But you also know I refuse to live even one day without you, Emerson. Deep down, you always knew you would end up wherever I was going to be."

Emerson didn't say anything for a few seconds, and even Roselyn seemed to accept their chosen fate, before Emerson turned to me. "Delaney?"

I looked into Emerson's rare silver eyes and told her the truth. "I registered Delaney for Blaineview the day I kicked Reynold's ass in front of the entire school, Em."

Roselyn's phone rang before anyone could comment on that bombshell. She pulled it out of her pocket and looked at the screen. "I don't recognize the number," she mumbled.

"It's probably one of those scam calls," Emerson predicted. "They're so damn annoying."

The phone went to voicemail, but then immediately started ringing again. And because Liam was just as much as a caveman as Ramsey, he grabbed Roselyn's phone out of her hand to answer the call from the unknown number. "Hello?" he barked, and Ramsey laughed. But that all changed as soon as Liam's back snapped straight, and he said, "Ava? Whoa, wait...yeah, okay...hold on."

I was already off the barstool and reaching for Linnie's phone as Liam handed it over to me. I put the phone up to my ear. "Ava?"

"Oh, thank God," she rushed out. "I didn't have your number or...anyone's. I...I had to get Roselyn's number from Cel-"

"Ava!" I barked. "What's wrong?"

"Yeah, yeah," she mumbled. "Sorry. Deke, it's Delaney-"

"What's wrong with Delaney?" Four little words, but they chilled the blood in my veins.

"I...*Christ.* I showed up to Trent White's party and...and I found Delaney here, Deke. I found her here, and she's drunk and...and I can't...she won't listen to me."

I could feel the chill in my bones turn into a white-hot anger that scared me a little. What in the fuck was Delaney doing at a party drunk? What was she trying to prove? I let her get away with calling in sick today for school, but had I known what I knew now, I'd have gone to her house and held her hostage until I got my point across that she belonged to me now.

"Watch her, Ava," I ordered. "I'm on my way." I hung up and when I looked up, I saw the worried faces of the girls, and the pissed off faces of the guys.

"How bad?" Liam asked.

"She's at Trent White's party and she's drunk," I said, barely managing to get the words out through my clenched teeth.

"Let's go," Ramsey said straightening up and ready to go.

"I think I'm going to fucking kill her," I muttered more to myself than the group.

"Hear her out, Deke," Roselyn implored.

I shot her a look. "And if she's with another guy?" I didn't wait for her answer. I just turned and headed out the door praying Ava's panic wasn't warranted, or else, God help Delaney Martin.

CHAPTER 16

Delaney ~

I was drunk.

I knew this.

I knew this but couldn't muster up the sense to care.

I had never planned on coming to Trent's party, but I had felt…restless all day long.

Like the coward I was becoming, I had called in sick to school today to avoid Deke. I had felt like I needed all the space I could get at his threat that tonight I'd be his. I was on edge, and I needed time to gather myself together. I knew Deke's words meant he planned on having sex with me, and while I wanted to, the anticipation was killing me.

I wasn't a femme fatal. I wasn't a sexy come-hither kind of temptress. How excited would he be when he realized I didn't know anything? It wasn't even my virginity that I was worried about. I still had that simply because I couldn't be bothered with dating. I've always been more interested in school and making something of myself, I really didn't care about dating around. Plus, getting to know people was just so…daunting. I hated doing it.

And if my anxiety hadn't already been sky high, Deke had sent me a text shortly after school had started telling me that he was granting me a pass because he knew I was nervous.

Granting me a pass.

The nerve.

At any rate, I had really planned on just staying home and throwing up from anxiousness, to the point where I'd just pass out, and Deke would have no choice but to leave me alone. However, my plans changed when Ava sent me a text that she might go to Trent's party if I didn't want to hang out tonight.

I had texted back that I was staying home, not ready to tell her about Deke, in case he didn't come over. But the more I thought about Ava and

Trent's party, the more I thought the party was a great idea.

I thought it was a great idea because, if Deke couldn't find me, well, that meant I could bide my time a little more. Deke would never think I'd be at Trent's party, or *any* party for that matter, so if I could avoid him for a little while longer...

And now I was here, drunk, and wondering where Ava was. I had texted her when I got here, but I hadn't heard from her and I couldn't find her anywhere. And because I was a loser with no friends, I had gone straight to the liquor to drink my awkwardness away until Ava got here.

"What the hell are you doing here?"

I was hiding out in the backyard, away from the crowd, when Winston's voice lashed out at me. I turned around to face him.

He looked awful.

"What the hell are *you* doing here?" I countered. "Shouldn't you be...I don't know. At home, resting or something?"

"My face is busted up, Delaney," he snapped. "It's not like my arms and legs don't work. I'm not an invalid. And what the fuck is that on your neck?" He gestured towards Deke's bite mark.

My brows shot up. Angry Winston was new. "I'm here to party," I said, ignoring his question.

He crossed his arms over his chest. "Since when do you party, Delaney?" He didn't give me a chance to answer. "Oh, I get it. You're hanging out with the cool kids now, and so, you think you need to party and get drunk to fit in. Is that it?"

I took a step back. "No," I snapped back. "They're not even here, you asshole. I'm here...I'm here just to have a good time. It's about time, don't you think?"

Winston's eyes searched mine. "No, Delaney. I don't think it's about time," he gritted through his teeth. "This isn't you."

"Maybe it is," I argued. "Maybe it's time to quit wasting my teenage years being your doormat."

"You've never been my doormat," he spat. "What the fuck has gotten into you?"

Good question.

The easy answer would be alcohol, but it wasn't that simple.

Deke Marlow is what has gotten into me. He's made me want new things, and it was messing up my entire identity. I was no longer the girl no one paid attention to. I was no longer the girl who was happy being in the library. I was no longer the girl who had her life mapped out for her with no worries.

I was a new Delaney Martin.

I was the Delaney Martin who wanted to be with Deke, knowing it was a bad idea.

I ignored his question and instead asked another one of my own. "Why d'you do it," I asked, jerking my head towards his face. "You had to know it wasn't going to end well for you, Winston. No one goes up against that group. *No one.*"

Whatever I was expecting him to say, the absolute truth wasn't it. I was sure Winston would make up some bullshit reason, but instead, he held truthful. "You're supposed to be my future, Delaney," he said. "Whether we love or hate each other, our futures have been tied together since we were ten. I really, really depended on you to be there in the end. Deke's threatening that."

I was probably too drunk to have this conversation, but we needed to have it. "How do you know it's not just some…passing fancy? Maybe Deke's just having fun, and…his interest will fizzle out in a couple of weeks. I mean, we still have college to get through."

His arms dropped to his sides. "If you think Deke's not in this for the long haul, you're not as smart as I always thought you were," he snorted. "Deke Marlow doesn't chase or claim girls, Delaney. The fact that he's done that with you means something."

"Even if that's true," I conceded, "what were you hoping to accomplish by challenging him in front of everyone?"

He shrugged a shoulder. "I thought maybe once he knew about us, he'd back off," he confessed. "Deke can have any girl he wants. He doesn't need to go after a girl who's already taken."

"But I was never really taken, Winston," I pointed out. "We had an agreement. It's not like we're in love with each other or have ever been in an actual relationship."

"Doesn't matter," he countered. "For all intents and purposes, you belong to me."

I took a swig of the vodka bottle I was holding and said the words I never thought I'd say. I said the words that were going to change everything, once and for all. "I *used* to belong to you, Winston," I said, feeling the words in my soul. "I think we both know that's changed."

"What happened to Deke only doing this for fun?" he challenged. "What happened to, we still have college to get through?"

"While that's all still true, Deke's irrelevant, Winston," I told him. "This isn't about him. This is about how I no longer want to wait in the wings until it's time to give in to our parents' demands."

"All of the sudden?" he barked.

"Yeah, all of the sudden," I barked back. "Even if Deke drops me tomorrow, I finally know what it feels like to be wanted and desired. I know what it feels like to *want* someone. There's no way I'm going back to settling for…nothing, while you continue to go out and get your kicks."

Winston threw up his hands in frustration. "So, then, we'll fucking date," he threw out.

I shook my head. "I don't want to date you, Winston," I said. "I don't *feel* for you other than a passing friendship, and I know you feel the same way about me. I *know* you do."

"But the plan-"

"Our *parents'* plan," I emphasized. "Not ours. It was never *ours.*"

He took a deep breath and said, "You're drunk, Delaney. I think we need to table this conversation for another time."

He was probably right, but I knew I'd still feel the same way later. Alcohol wasn't making me say all these things. Alcohol was just making me say it without consequence for what my words meant. And they meant a great deal of change and unpleasantness for our parents. My words were going to ruin their plans for a future dynasty between our two families. My words were changing the direction of so many lives, and alcohol was making me not give a shit.

"Maybe you're right," I conceded. I patted him on his chest. "I'm off to go dance, drink, and forget that you and Deke Marlow exist." It'd be easy to forget Winston existed, but I suspected forgetting Deke would take some more alcohol. Maybe a lobotomy even.

"Delaney, let me take you home," Winston replied. "You don't belong here."

I knew I didn't, but go big or go home, right?

I needed to…not be shy, quiet, nerdy Delaney. It was the only way I was going to be brave enough to sleep with Deke. It was the only way I was going to be able to sleep with him without him crushing everything good in me. I had to prove I could party and be cool and popular. I had to prove I was just as strong as Ava, Emerson, and Roselyn.

I couldn't be meek Delaney Martin. Deke would crush me if I didn't form a stronger backbone. He would run over me if I didn't…

Oh, who was I kidding? Deke Marlow was going to own and devastate me.

CHAPTER 17

Deke ~

I'm not sure how many traffic laws I broke getting to Trent's house, but with every passing minute I could feel my mind splintering with all kinds of unpleasant possibilities as to why Delaney had gone to a party without Ava.

And worse? What was she doing that Ava said she couldn't get Delaney to listen to her?

I knew Delaney was nervous about this weekend. I knew my words had put her on edge. When I realized she hadn't shown up to school this morning, I hadn't really been surprised. I also didn't think any less of her. I knew I was...a lot. I knew I intimidated people, and I knew I Delaney's personality was...not compatible with mine if you did the math, but I didn't care.

Delaney was mine.

My car was barely in park before I was turning it off and out of the driver's side door. Everyone else had followed in Ramsey's Range Rover and I could hear the car doors opening and closing behind me. Whatever awaited me in that house, I knew it wouldn't be anything that couldn't be handled by the five of us, even if it meant bloody killing someone.

As I stormed into the house, I turned my head back and told Linnie, "Call Ava and ask her where the fuck they are."

I turned back around and started scanning the foyer and passing through it to the living room. I kept scanning and scanning, but I didn't see her. Finally, Roselyn piped up, "They're in the backyard. They're on the decking."

Without any 'excuse me's or 'pardon me's, we swept through the house towards the backyard. I wasn't sure what I was expecting, but never in a million years would I have imagined the sight that greeted me when I cleared the back sliding glass door. Christina Aguilera was blaring through the surround sound speakers talking about wanting to be dirty and there was Delaney Martin dancing like she was auditioning for a goddamn music video.

I heard a low whistle behind me. "Where in the hell did she even learn how to dance like that?" Liam exclaimed right before he let out a whoosh from Roselyn elbowing him no doubt.

Delaney was dancing alone, but she was moving her body *not* like a goddamn virgin, that's for sure. I stood stunned at the way she was moving, the bottle of liquor in her hand, the fucking outfit that was not covering shit, and how flushed her face was, but I had no idea if it was from the alcohol or the dancing.

Her hair was down, flying all around her, and she was wearing a tight green tank top, a white loose skirt that stopped mid-thigh, and some white sandals, and none of it hid her assets.

But what was killing me?

The pink blush of color in her face was making the scar across her cheek whiter. It was making it stand out, and for whatever reason, *that's* what was getting my dick hard. I thought it'd be my mark, but it wasn't.

That fucking scar.

That fucking scar that proved there was more to Delaney Martin than the quiet library book nerd we all thought her to be all these years.

Before I could go over and drag her away, Ava rushed up to us. "Oh, thank God!" she cried. I looked down at her and her face was full of worry and wariness. "She's drunk, Deke. She's drunk, and she had texted me and I didn't get the text..." Ava shook her head. "Who cares? She's drunk and you need to go get her. She won't listen to me."

"What the fuck is she doing here?" Ramsey asked from behind me.

Ava glanced over at him and her face blanched. I suppose the sight of all of us here to get Delaney was a bit overwhelming. "I...I don't know," she answered. "I told her I might be here, so...she might have meant to meet me here. I don't know..."

"What did she say when you saw her?" Roselyn asked.

"She just keeps saying she's here to party," Ava rushed out, worried and...well, worried. "And I don't know what the fuck that means. Delaney doesn't party."

My eyes shot back to where Delaney was dancing and, suddenly, I knew what she was doing here. She was hiding from me. She was here because she didn't think I'd ever think to look for her here. She was hiding from what was happening between us.

Delaney was trying to make sense of the changes happening in her life and she was doing what all idiotic teenage kids do when they're confused. She was drinking and dancing her problems away. Too bad I was her biggest problem and nothing she could do would push me away.

I glanced back down at Ava. "She's going to be pissed that you called me. You know that, right?"

I realized there was more to Ava than I had ever given her credit for when she said, "I know she is." She shook her head again. "I know Delaney's going to feel betrayed and hurt that I...I didn't pick her side this time. I know that,

Deke, but…" I watched as Ava stood to her full height, and I realized she was struggling with upsetting the only real friend she's ever had. "But her safety and…her reputation are more important than how much she might hate me for this. She can hate me for the rest of our lives, and I can live with that, if she's safe and…no one talks about her like she's…trash."

We all stood there and even with the party all around us, you could *feel* how much Ava loved Delaney. Whatever we ever suspected about their friendship, Ava's declaration proved that I'd never have to worry about Delaney when she was with Ava. Ava would never let her reputation or wild ways taint Delaney in any way.

"Deke, check it out," Liam said.

I looked over at Delaney and I saw some guy walking up to her to dance. And, while that had me already balling up my fists, that was nothing compared to seeing Winston come into view. He looked pissed, and he was walking towards Delaney to get her away from the guy wanting to dance with her.

Oh, fuck no.

Delaney was mine.

She was mine, and I'd be goddamned if I'll let another guy claim or defend her in front of me. Winston was striding up towards them like he had the right to pull her away from the guy, and he didn't.

I took off, and luckily for him, I beat him to it. But it had been close. We stood on either side of Delaney, staring each other down, the guy who was going to dance with her was long gone.

I snatched Delaney by her arm and yanked her towards me. "Can I help you, Reynolds?"

The guy's face was all busted up, and he knew he couldn't beat me, but he didn't back down and I grudgingly respected that. "I'm not going to fade into the background so that she can be with you if you're *not* going to take care of her, Marlow," he snapped. He threw his arm up, indicating the party. "Because this is *not* taking care of her. Delaney doesn't belong here. If you were doing your job, she wouldn't be here!"

I wanted to kill him.

I wanted to kill him, but he wasn't wrong.

"Oh, hey!" Delaney's drunk ass piped up. "I am my own woman, damn it!" She tried to wrench her arm free of my grasp, but that wasn't happening. "I don't need a man, and I sure as hell don't need either of you to be the man I need, if I needed one."

Christ, she was drunk.

She whirled around towards Winston. "For years, you've known we were supposed to get married, and you spent all these years offering me passive acknowledgement, at best. We were friends when we were little, but as soon as you discovered teenage pussy, I wasn't even that anymore. And now you want to give a shit? Fuck that, Winston."

I was next.

Delaney whirled around towards me and let loose. "And you," she scoffed. "For years you never even knew I existed. And if you did, you didn't care one way or the other. Suddenly, I fascinate you, and because you're bored with your endless buffet of pussy and ass, you want a challenge and have decided that I'm it." She didn't know how wrong she was. "I'm here because of *you*, Deke," she punctuated. "I'm here to see what if feels like to be cool and popular. I'm here because the real me can't possibly hold your interest for long, and for some fucked-up reason, I want that. I want you to want me, but I want you to want me for longer than it takes for you to win. I'm not the girl for you. I'm not even *close* to the kind of girl you're used to." Her hand scanned down her body like she was presenting herself. "This is the kind of girl you like, right? And this is the kind of girl who is brave enough to do...what you want her to do."

This conversation wasn't for Winston's ears. "Let's go, Delaney," I replied. "You're drunk and don't know what you're saying."

She let out a bitter laugh. "I know *exactly* what I'm saying," she argued. "I'm saying that you and Winston can go fuck yourselves."

"Delaney-"

My eyes shot over towards Reynolds. "Don't," I snapped. "Do fucking not, Reynolds. This isn't your business."

"It is if she doesn't want to be with you either," he snapped back.

Like fucking hell she didn't want to be with me.

CHAPTER 18

Delaney

All that booze, and for what?

Standing in Deke's house-sober as a goat-I was feeling miserable.

After I had told both Deke and Winston to go fuck themselves, I had been feeling rather proud of myself, but that had faded quickly when Deke had let go of my arm and had reached for Winston. Suddenly, we had been surrounded by Liam, Ramsey, Emerson, Roselyn, and Ava, and the guys had restrained Deke, while the girls had surrounded me.

I wasn't sure why Winston kept antagonizing Deke, but I suspected it was to prove the point that he was still dedicated to our arrangement even after telling him I no longer cared to go through with it. But, whatever his reasons, I needed to cement my decision before Deke ended up killing Winston, and that meant telling our parents.

After Liam and Ramsey separated Deke and Winston, Deke had grabbed me by my arm and drug me behind him through the house and to his car. He had tossed me into the passenger seat, buckled me in, and took off from Trent's. Halfway down the road though, I had gotten sick and Deke had had to pull over so I could throw up the twenty gallons of vodka I had consumed.

Okay, maybe it hadn't been twenty gallons, but I didn't drink. And because I didn't drink, a half bottle of vodka was equivalent to twenty gallons in my mind.

When I had fallen out of the car, I had ran behind a random tree that lined the sidewalk and, while I was heaving up my innards, Deke had come around, held my hair and rubbed my back all the while telling me what an idiot I was.

Yep.

No sweet, soothing words of love from Deke Marlow.

Once my stomach was empty, and I was thoroughly embarrassed, he had put me back into the car and we drove the rest of the way to his house in silence. And, now, I was standing in his living room, sober, and I could feel a headache coming on the size of Texas.

This was not what I had in mind when I had gone to Trent's.

Deke was shutting and locking the door behind us, and I was too miserable to even worry about being alone with him in his house. A girl who doesn't drink should never pop her party cherry with a bottle of hard liquor. Suddenly, I wasn't feeling as smart as my IQ and good grades indicated.

"Come on," Deke barked as he grabbed my hand and pulled me behind him.

I followed because I seriously didn't have the physical or mental strength to battle him. Why did people do this? I wasn't even experiencing a next day hang over yet, and I didn't want to.

Once we walked up the stairs to his bedroom, he left me standing in the middle of the room as he pulled a shirt from his closet. "Deke-"

"Don't, Delaney," he snapped. "I'm one irritated nerve away from laying you across my lap and spanking the shit out of you like an out-of-control child." My lips curled in and I wisely kept my mouth shut. He thrust his shirt in my hands and pushed at me until we were both walking into his en suite bathroom.

I looked around and the bathroom matched his bedroom with the dark black and grey tiles. His bedroom had light grey walls, a dark grey bed set, and black furniture. It all looked very sleek and expensive. His car was white, so I never expected his room to be decorated in dark colors. Uh, not that I had given his bedroom much thought, that is.

I stayed silent as I watched Deke yank open a drawer and pull out a value pack of toothbrushes. He pulled one out and dumped it next to his in the toothbrush holder. "Take a shower, brush your teeth, and do whatever else it is you do to get ready for bed, and then come back into the bedroom," he grumbled.

"Deke-" I tried again.

"Goddamn it, Delaney," he barked. "Another word and I swear to God..."

"Sorry," I mumbled, properly chastised. I stayed where I was as Deke took two towels from a built-in cabinet next to the shower and placed them on the counter. The second he walked out of the room, I locked the door and started to take off the ridiculous clothes I had on. They weren't even my real clothes. They were an old outfit that my mother had bought me one day while in Paris. She thought it was cute, but it had just been further proof that she didn't know me at all.

I undressed, turned on the shower and got in, letting the warm water sooth away all my bad decisions from tonight. It wasn't until I reached for the shampoo that I realized I was going to smell like Deke, and that realization had my tummy feeling hollow.

It felt hollow because I liked that idea.

I showered and used Deke's shampoo, conditioner, and body wash and I felt like such a girl afterwards. When I stepped out of the shower, dried off, and then put on his shirt, the feeling had intensified. Deke's shirt fell all the way to my knees, and it felt like such a girlfriend thing to be wearing his clothes.

I brushed the hell out of my teeth and tongue until I felt all my vodka regret scrubbed away. After that, I searched the drawers for something to brush my hair. I found a brush and took my time detangling my hair. After I was done, I looked into the mirror and gave myself the biggest pep talk in history.

Finally, I unlocked the door and walked out to find Deke sitting on his bed, watching TV, in a pair of basketball shorts and nothing more.

Sweet Christ.

He stood up and I couldn't help but notice he still looked pissed. I felt stupid saying, "Uhm, I don't have my purse with me or anything, so…uh, I don't have a scrunchie for my hair…"

Deke placed his hands on his hips, looked up towards the ceiling, and let out a breath so deep, I could hear it clear across the room. He didn't say anything as he brought his head back down, gave me a quick look, and then walked out of the room.

Well.

I sat on his bed because I didn't want to add to my nerd status by just standing around looking like a dweeb. I had no idea where he'd gone to, but if he was as pissed off as he claimed, it was quite possible he left me here to just go to sleep.

A couple of minutes later, Deke returned with a scrunchie, and my heart dropped. *This asshole was giving me a scrunchie that belonged to another girl.* A scrunchie another girl left at his house. Maybe it was the alcohol, maybe it was the stress of this past week, maybe it was dealing with Winston, the overwhelming association with Deke's friends…whatever it was, I could feel the tingle in my nose that suggested tears were about to make an appearance.

Who does that?

Who gives a girl another girl's property? I mean, that takes insensitivity to an entirely different level.

I stood up, and he reached out to hand me the scrunchie. "Uhm, no thank you," I mumbled. I may feel…defeated whenever I was around Deke, but I wasn't a complete weakling. And I would not be wearing anything one of his other conquests left behind.

Deke smirked, and I wanted to do him violence. I'd never been particularly physical or violent before, but Deke brought out that side of me. He made my irritation levels skyrocket, and it's like I wanted to take out every life frustration I've ever had out on him.

"My hair can just-"

"It's Emerson's or Roselyn's," he said. "There's a shitload of them in the game room."

I could feel my face flush with embarrassment at my presumptions about what went on in his house. I reached out and took the scrunchie. "Thanks," I mumbled.

He crossed his arms over his chest before saying, "I've never had a girl over here, Delaney. Except for Em and Linnie, you're the only girl who's ever been to my house."

Em and Linnie?

The personalization caused butterflies to take up residence in my stomach. Saying his nicknames for Emerson and Roselyn was taking this to a seriously personal level. Deke's reputation preceded him, so I didn't consider anything we've done sexually as personal. He hadn't done to me anything he hadn't done with a dozen other girls. But using Emerson's and Roselyn's nicknames with me was super personal.

After throwing my hair up in a wet bun, I shrugged a shoulder and said, "It's none of my business who's been here and who hasn't."

Deke stepped to me and he made sure to scan the length of my body before his eyes settled on mine. "Everything that has to do with me is now your business, Lamb," he replied.

I decided to test him.

"Okay," I challenged. "So, then, are the rumors about you, Liam, and Roselyn true?" His face became an instant mask. "So, then, I guess everything that has to do with you *isn't* my business."

He looked down at me and I knew immediately where I stood with him, and it was *behind* Ramsey, Liam, Emerson, and Roselyn. Deke might want to sleep with me, but I was beginning to realize that my assumption about being a challenge was spot on.

"Don't ever ask me about Roselyn again," he said impassively-*emotionlessly*.

I was such a goddam fool.

CHAPTER 19

Deke ~

I never imagined I could feel so many different emotions all in one night.

I had gone from cool, and chillin' at Ramsey's, to frantic and worried when Ava called, to surprised at seeing Delaney drunk and dancing, to pissed off and wanting to kill Reynolds again, to sympathy when Delaney had thrown up everywhere, to anxiousness when I finally got her back to my place, to irritated when she tried to explain herself, to horny when I thought about her naked in my shower, to consumed when she had walked out of the bathroom in only my shirt, to tired when she quietly mumbled that she didn't have a hair tie, to cocky at her jealousy when she thought the hair tie belonged to another girl, to raging mad when she had asked about Roselyn.

A couple of months ago, a video of Roselyn and Liam having sex surfaced where Liam explained, quite clearly in the recording, how I had been an extra in the bedroom. That video and the person who took it had been taken care of, but while no one outside our group had seen the video, rumors of its existence had still started. We all had done our best to shut the rumors down, but there were still mumbles here and there.

Last year, Liam, Roselyn, and I had entered into a ménage relationship that lasted about a year. It had been born out of the need to protect Roselyn from her fuck of a stepbrother, but it had grown into love for Liam and Roselyn. And for me, Linnie had become one of my closest friends. And as much as I cared about Delaney, I would not be telling that story. It was Roselyn's story to tell, and if she never felt comfortable with Delaney enough to tell her, well, then, so be it.

There was also the issue of Delaney's take on the truth. Would she be jealous of Roselyn? Would she insist I could no longer be friends with her? And, if she did, how big of a hypocrite would I be when I wanted Delaney nowhere near Winston and she hadn't even slept with him?

I could admit I was at a loss on how to handle this, but I knew I'd never betray Roselyn and Liam by sharing a secret that wasn't mine alone to share. So, I switched gears. "What were you doing at Trent's party tonight, Delaney?"

She sat back on my bed, and no lie, seeing her on my bed was fucking with me. I hadn't lied when I told her I'd never brought a girl here. Even when I was sleeping with Roselyn, we hooked up at her house or Liam's, but mostly at her house. It was easier to pass our cars off in her driveway as that we were there to see her stepbrother, Brandon. Roselyn didn't have a reason to be at mine or Liam's house.

Delaney looked up at me from the bed and hit me with the truth. "I was trying to forget the clusterfuck you've turned my life into," she replied. "I was also hoping to hide from you a little longer." So, I was right. She had been avoiding tonight.

I stepped towards her until I was standing right in front of her and she was forced to open her legs so I could fit in between them. I stared down at her and it wasn't lost on me that she was in the perfect position to suck my dick. Suddenly, the night of the beach party came back and the look on Delaney's face as Melissa sucked me dry.

I had never wanted a blowjob from a girl so badly in all my life.

It was all I could do to focus on our conversation, but I did my best. "Why?" I asked. "You already know how this is going to pan out."

She shook her head. "It's so easy for you, because you're used to taking whatever it is you want," she said. "My...decision to be with you affects more than just if I orgasm." I didn't like how she was reducing what we had to the basics of sex, but I let her continue. "I have to deal with Winston and the fallout from our parents now that...now that I've changed my mind about marrying him."

Delaney will never know what her words have affected. "What's the worst that can happen?"

"Oh, I don't know," she deadpanned. "Maybe not pay for my college? Maybe disown me? Kick me out of my home?"

I reared back. "All that just because you don't want to marry Reynolds anymore?"

"That arrangement wasn't made out of some deep-seated need to see Winston and me happy in life, Deke," she sneered. "That arrangement was made so our parents' businesses could combine and become a medical powerhouse. Do you honestly think they're going to take kindly to me messing that up for them? Especially, since I've gone along with their plans all these years?"

She had a point.

She had a point, and if her parents were like the rest of the parents of Sands Cove, her happiness *wasn't* paramount to what they wanted from her.

I reached down, cupped her face in my left hand, and all thoughts of her parents and Reynolds vanished. Besides, her parents' retaliation wouldn't matter in the scheme of things because it was now my job to take care of Delaney. And that included paying for college or moving her in if she did get kicked out of her house. Hell, I'll probably move her in with me any damn way. Roselyn lived with Liam, and Emerson lived with Ramsey, so why wouldn't Delaney live with me? We were all legal adults, after all. And all those thoughts made me realize I was tired of waiting.

"Are you still scared?" I asked even though it wouldn't matter. I was taking Delaney tonight, and I didn't care if she was an emotional wreck. I probably should, but Delaney showing up at Trent's party showed me just how much I needed to lock her down and put an end to her...indecisiveness.

She didn't avert her eyes. "I'm not sure," she admitted. "I think...my problem is with what comes afterwards."

I ran my thumb across her lower lip, and I could feel my dick rising. I wanted inside her pussy like I wanted to take my next breath, but I wanted her lips wrapped around my cock more. I wanted her to fulfill her fantasy from that night in the trees. And it didn't matter that she's never given head before. I knew-I absolutely *knew* her lips wrapped around me was going to be the best thing to ever happen to me.

Motherfucker.

I was in love with fucking Delaney Martin.

I knew I wanted her. I knew I was going to have her. I knew I craved her and wouldn't be without her as long as she called to me. But I knew it was love because I knew she could give me the worst blowjob in history right now, but because it was her...because *it was her*, it'd be the best I ever had.

Delaney would be the best *everything* I would ever have.

"Do you want to know what comes afterwards?" I asked. "Because I'll be happy to tell you, Lamb."

Then she did something I hadn't anticipated.

Delaney opened her lips and took my thumb into her mouth. Her gaze never wavered as she flicked her tongue around the tip of my digit. "Are you sure?" I asked. "I need you to be sure, and I need you to say the words, Delaney. I need the words because I won't stop once I get started, and you won't be able to stop me or change your mind."

She pushed my thumb out of her mouth with her tongue. I watched as she took a deep breath before saying the words that would change both our lives forever. "I'm yours," she whispered. "I'm yours until you're done with me, Deke."

The relief that left my lungs was palpable. "I'll never be done with you, baby," I told her honestly. I should have told her I loved her, but I knew she wasn't ready to hear that. I knew she was already feeling overwhelmed, if I told her I loved her now, she'd freak the fuck out.

She gave me a small nod, but it wasn't enough. "I need the words, Delaney," I repeated.

I watched her take a deep breath and then she said, "I want this, Deke. I want *you*."

"Tell me," I ordered. "Tell me what you want, Lamb."

Her chocolate orbs shot towards my groin and then back up again. "You were right that night, you know," she whispered. "I was watching Melissa, and I had wished it was me on my knees." My heart felt like it was going to beat clean out of my chest at her confession. "She looked...she looked powerful down on her knees like that. I saw your hands tighten in her hair and I thought it was...thrilling to be able to control a guy from that submissive position." I wanted to yank her up and kiss the fuck out of her, but I didn't want to interrupt her struggling confession. "And then...when I looked up and saw you looking at me..." Delaney took another deep breath. "...I wanted to be the one who put that look on your face."

I huffed and told her a confession of my own. "You *are* the one who put that look on my face," I admitted. "My hands tightened in her hair because I had been looking at *you*, Delaney. Watching *you* is what made me cum, not her."

Her face looked...eager. She looked like she wished for those words to be the absolute truth; and they were. She'd never know how true every word I've spoken to her was. "I...I want to..." Her face turned bright red, and I loved how her party-girl experiment went south.

I decided to help her out a bit. "You wanna suck my dick, baby?"

Delaney's eyes dilated and her eyes looked like melted chocolate, dreamy and soft. "I...won't know what I'm doing though."

I cradled her face again. "Don't worry about that," I replied. "I'll tell you what do you, Lamb."

"I want you, Deke," she repeated.

"You have me, Delaney," I promised.

CHAPTER 20

Delaney ~

I've never been so scared in my life.

Even when my parents held me down and sliced my face open, I hadn't been this scared. Maybe it was because I had no idea what my parents had been about until it was too late. I remember being scared at being held down, but they were my parents. My parents would never hurt me, right?

Wrong.

So, so very wrong.

Before fear could set in, agonizing pain had ripped through my body. From there, the pain had morphed into incredulousness at what my parents had done. Even at such a young age, I knew that what they had done to me was not normal.

It wasn't love.

But this?

I had been resigned to the fact that I'd eventually end up here with Deke, and as much as I tried to fight it, I wanted Deke. It was the turmoil that was to come that I didn't want to deal with.

But what frightened me now?

There was no way I would be able to keep Deke's interest after tonight. I had no clue what to do in bed besides the basic mechanics of sex. I knew the gist of how to give a blowjob. I knew that a guy used his tongue when he went down on a girl. I knew the penis went into the vagina. I knew the mechanics, but I didn't know how to...inspire passion.

Oh, I knew his dick was hard, but Deke was a healthy, hot-blooded male. For all I knew, that hard dick of his could be for anyone who was sitting on his bed. I wasn't important to him no matter what bullshit he sprouted. He made that clear when he told me never to question him about Roselyn again. I might...matter, but I wasn't important.

So, what scared me?

I knew after tonight, my life would change drastically, and not necessarily *for* Deke, but because of Deke.

There would no longer be Winston as my safety net because after tonight, a passionless marriage would no longer be enough for me. There would be a shift in my relationship with my parents because I would no longer be a part of their plan. Now, while they neglected me for the most part, the shift would come in the form of their purse strings. I knew this. There was also the fact that I'd no longer be able to live in ignorance. I would know passion. I would know lust. I would know what it feels like to be owned by another human being. I would finally know what I was missing, and I was scared that Deke would take what he could and walk away when there was nothing left for him to take; nothing left for me to give to someone else.

I knew all this, but none of it was going to stop me, anyway.

I lowered my eyes and reached for the waistband of his basketball shorts. I tugged them down and his erection sprang free and bounced against his body. The tinted skin looked painfully stretched tight, and I could feel the heat graze my face, but that was nothing when I took in how big he was.

Even being a virgin, I knew Deke was huge.

I took a deep breath as I wrapped my hand around his dick, and it surprised me how hot it was. I mean, I guess it made sense with all the blood flowing through it, I...just wasn't expecting it. Deke let out a quiet hiss above me and that gave me the courage to move forward with my decision to give him this.

Give him *me*.

I leaned forward and there was a drop of pre-cum on the tip, so I decided to start there. I lick the tip and Deke's hands shot into my hair, holding on tightly. The feeling took me back to the night on the beach and I could feel myself becoming wet with need. I opened my mouth and took Deke to the back of my throat.

Now, while I wasn't a professional, I knew enough not to use my teeth, and I knew enough that the deeper the better. So, I grabbed the base of his dick and swallowed him down, and I couldn't believe how turned on I was becoming from doing something that, in theory, should be for his pleasure only.

"Fuck, Lamb," Deke muttered, "you're sucking me so good, baby."

I wasn't sure if I really was or if he was just saying that to encourage me, but it...helped. I took him as deep as I could, and when I felt him hit the back of my throat, I pulled back. His hands tightened in my hair with each dive down my throat and I realized I was right. Pulling this kind of need out of him felt powerful. Deke was standing over me, but I felt like I had the power here. I felt like I could ask him for anything, and he'd give it as long as I kept sucking his dick.

After a while, with short labored breaths, he warned, "Baby, I'm going to cum if you keep that up."

Did I want that? Did I want my first time to be so…*filthy?*

Yes. Yes, I did.

I started moving faster, using my hand to help stimulate the length of him that I couldn't get into my mouth. Deke was long and thick, and even using my hand, I still couldn't wrap around him completely. I knew he was going to tear me in half, but I couldn't bring myself to care. I wanted him. I wanted him so much, I was going to let my first blowjob end with swallowing his seed.

"Lamb," he breathed. "Delaney, baby? I'm going to cum…"

I held on.

I held on and tightened my grip and my lips around him until he let out a deep moan and shot his orgasm down my throat. I kept my lips firmly wrapped around him as he shot squirt after squirt in my mouth. His hands were fisted in my hair as I swallowed every drop. It was intense. It was exciting. And it was forever.

This was forever.

I will forever remember this first.

I will forever remember this night.

I will forever remember Deke.

He pulled away from me, and when I glanced up, he looked absolutely wrecked. It was pathetic, but I wanted some praise. I wanted some…something.

Deke grabbed me by my shoulders and hauled me to my feet as he bounced his legs, making his shorts fall all the rest of the way down. He cradled my face and slammed his lips down on mine as he stepped from the puddle of his shorts. He was completely naked, but he was kissing me so thoroughly, I couldn't even appreciate the view.

When he was done kissing me, he pulled back and said, "Now, it's my turn."

Remembering I was naked underneath his shirt, I didn't have time for modesty as Deke grabbed the hem of his shirt and whipped it over my head. I stood before Deke Marlow completely naked, and I was so insecure about this revelation, I couldn't even take this chance to finally take in a naked Deke Marlow.

"D…De…Deke…" I couldn't do anything about the tremor in my voice. I was nervous, and I wasn't going to pretend to be otherwise. Deke smirked, and I wanted to bash his head in. It reminded me of just how comfortable he was in this kind of situation, and the hit to my self-esteem was hard and accurate. "You don't get to laugh at me, Deke," I snapped.

His arm snaked out, and he fisted his hand in my hair as he pulled my head back, forcing me to look up at him. I watched as his eyes stared at my lips and slowly made their way down my naked body. It was a horribly tense few seconds before his eyes made their way back up to mine.

Deke's green gaze was blazing as he asked, "You think I'm laughing at you?" When I didn't answer fast enough, he shook my head in his grasp. "Do you think I'm laughing at you?"

"I...I don't know..." I admitted.

His expression looked thunderous. "Why would you think I'd be *laughing* at you?"

My left hand latched onto his waist as my right hand shot back to wrap around the arm of the hand he had fisted in my hair. He was tightening his hold, and it was beginning to hurt. "Bec...because I don't know what I'm doing," I confessed.

Deke looked sinister, and his voice was rough and raw, but it didn't match his words. "Lamb, if that was you not knowing what you're doing, then I'm fucked when you finally do know," he growled.

That was it.

That was the praise I had been looking for, but it was cut short when he said, "You say you don't know what you're doing, but if that were the case, then why do I want to wait to taste your pussy for another time, and just throw you on the bed and fuck you until you bleed all over me?"

Holy shit. "Deke..."

"If you don't know what you're doing, then why do I want to forget that this is your first time, and fuck you like a dirty slut?" He asked, making my center throb and my knees weak. "Why do you have my dick harder than it's *ever fucking been*, Delaney, if you don't know what you're doing?"

"I can still taste you on my tongue," I whispered, not knowing exactly why I said that.

Deke leaned down until I could feel his breath on my face. "By the time I'm done with you, Delaney, you're going have the taste, feel, and scent of my cum all over your body, baby."

Well, damn.

CHAPTER 21

Deke ~

If I hadn't seen with my own two eyes just how nervous Delaney had been, and still was, I would never have guessed that had been her first blowjob. Delaney had sucked my cock like she had been inside my head. She mastered every stroke to make me erupt in her mouth quicker than I've ever had.

And I had been right.

It had been the best head of my life.

And now? Now, all I wanted to do was tear into her. I wanted to fuck her, and I don't mean just fuck her. I wanted to *rut* her. I wanted to sink my teeth in the back of her neck and draw blood as she came on my cock. I wanted to own her. I wanted to possess her.

I wanted to fucking hurt her.

My dark side, the one that I worked to hide so well, had been unleashed. *She* had unleashed it.

I know now that Delaney had unleashed it the night at the beach. It had just been biding its time until she granted me permission to use her.

To love her.

And I planned on beating into her body until she begged me to stop, but as much as I was primed and ready to go, I needed to prepare her. I knew this. I knew I couldn't let loose just yet. She'd never let me near her again if I didn't bring her *some* pleasure.

I released my hold in her hair and told her, "Get on the bed."

"Deke..." she pleaded.

"Get on the fucking bed, Delaney," I snapped.

I watched her crazy-sexy body run to the side of the bed, yank the covers back, and hide underneath. I stalked towards her and her face was a beautiful blush as she took in my naked body. I got into bed and climbed over her. I braced all my weight on my elbows as I looked down at her.

Delaney looked terrified and my dick started to harden again. "Tell me again," I demanded.

Her big brown eyes searched mine. "I want you," she surrendered.

My lips touched her scar, and I went from there and started working my way down her body. She let out soft moans and whimpers as I traveled over her skin. When my face got to her big tits, I did what I've been wanting to do since forever; I grabbed her left tit and started sucking on her light pink nipple. It was hard and waiting for me.

"Oh, God..." she mewled as her hands sunk into my hair.

I turned to her right tit and gave it the same attention. Her skin tasted clean, and she smelled like my body wash and that was fucking me up something fierce. When I was done with her tits, I kept traveling south, anticipation coursing through my every nerve at finally finding out what Delaney's pussy would taste like. "Spread your legs for me, baby," I cajoled. I wasn't going to take her slowly, but I needed everything, before I sunk my dick into her, to be perfect for her. I needed her body soaking wet with release and I needed her mind unable to think behind the pleasure I was giving her.

Delaney's legs opened for me, and soon I was nestled in between her smooth, creamy thighs. The second her scent hit my nostrils I knew what it felt like to be a drug addict. I knew I was going to move her in tomorrow because there's no way I was going to live without her next to me every night.

Resting the weight of my shoulders on the inside of her thighs, I used my hands to spread her smooth pussy lips open and took that first swipe at euphoria, and Delaney tasted every bit as delicious as I knew she would.

"Oh, my God, Deke..." she cried, her hands flying over her to grab onto the headboard. Delaney had a tight trimmed triangle above her clit, but the rest of her was bare, and so it was easier to eat and lick her everywhere.

And I did.

I devoured her.

I made out with her pussy and it wasn't until she gave up that first orgasm that I finally sunk my fingers into her pussy, and it was just as tight was the last time they were in her wet cunt. I turned the upward and massaged that spot that so many guys don't have the patience to look for.

Or they were just fucking tools and couldn't find it.

I pulled my face away from Delaney's pussy longer enough to demand, "Give me another, baby. Soak my fucking face."

She moaned and her hips started to match the rhythm of my fingers. I kept my tongue on her clit as my fingers worked her pussy and, soon enough, she was giving me her second cum of the night. But I needed one more. I seriously needed her soaked to prevent any serious damage to her body. Not trying to brag, but The Lord blessed me, and He wasn't stingy about it.

After tearing another orgasm from Delaney, I wiped my face on the inside of her right thigh and kissed my way back up her body. When I reached her face, she looked sated and ready to pass out, and it was exactly how I needed her.

Because my dick was harder than iron, I didn't have to use my hand to guide the head towards her opening. I braced myself on my elbows, started down at a very high-looking Delaney, and slammed my cock balls deep inside her unused body with one thrust.

"Deke!" she screamed as she threw her head back and her hands fisted the sheet on either side of us.

I was such a bastard.

I've always been a bastard and have always taken what I wanted. But, never in my life, have I ever wanted something like I wanted Delaney. So, instead of going slow, instead of giving her time to adjust, instead of making this special for her, I drilled into her like she was a seasoned pro. "Fuck, Lamb," I grunted. "You're so fucking tight."

"Deke, it hurts," she cried, and it was like music to my ears.

"I know. I know, and it's going to keep hurting because I can't fucking stop, Delaney," I panted, breaking the news to her. "I'm not going to stop fucking you, baby. Not until you cum all over my cock and milk me dry."

"Oh, God…" she whimpered.

Delaney was in pain. She was fisting the sheets. She had tears leaking down the side of her face. She was moaning and whimpering. But most importantly? She wasn't telling me to stop.

She was taking every hard thrust into her body and her hips were pushing back, and I knew why. She had mentioned how Melissa had looked powerful on her knees, and I knew my loss of control was Delaney's way of feeling powerful. She wasn't going to tell me to stop because she wanted to break me. She wanted to give as good as she got. My weakness was her aphrodisiac.

Delaney wanted me at her mercy, and I was there.

She felt like absolute Heaven with her pussy wrapped so tightly around my cock, and I knew I'd never get enough of this. I knew, now, why Ramsey and Liam had such a connection with Em and Linnie. Looking down, and seeing Delaney's virgin blood all over me, was enough to make me want to stay buried in her every minute of every day. Even my bite mark on her neck hadn't brought out this kind of possessiveness. Delaney was officially mine now, and that knowledge had me ramming my cock into her so hard, I knew we were both going to be sporting bruises.

"You're mine, Delaney," I grunted. "Say it."

Her legs opened wider and, instead, she said, "I…I think I'm going to cum again, Deke."

"Fucking say it!" I barked.

"Yours," she moaned hysterically. "I'm yours."

I braced my weight on the flat of my hands and fucked Delaney like I was going insane; and I think I was. "Cum on my cock, baby," I begged. "I want to see your blood and our cum on my cock."

"Oh, Jesus..." she groaned, and then her hands latched onto my arms as she threw her head back and came all over me.

Her pussy's contractions around my dick were enough to set me off. I came with a force that almost put my back out.

But I didn't stop.

I didn't stop slamming into Delaney until my dick started to soften. I made sure every last drop of my seed was nestled deep inside her womb. When I did finally pull out, I fell onto my back and pulled her to me. I felt her hot tears on my chest, but I didn't ask about them. Nor did I hurry to clean us up. I liked us laying there dirty with one another.

After a few minutes, I asked that one question that needed to be asked, "Delaney, are you on birth control?"

Her body shot up and the gasp that escaped her was loud enough to be heard downstairs. She looked down at me, eyes wide and face pale. "You...you didn't...you didn't use a condom?"

I smirked and shook my head. "Nope," I admitted. "And I'm not ever going to."

CHAPTER 22

Delaney ~

My body felt like I'd been run over by a bus. Even though we were only able to have sex three times throughout the night, my body felt like it had been taken a million times over.

Because Deke hadn't been slow or tender, in the least, my body had shut down after only three times. There was no longer any pleasure towards the end and that's when he finally took mercy on me.

But Holy Bejesus, those first two times? Oh, there had been pain, quite a bit of it actually, but the pleasure? The pleasure had been overwhelming enough to ignore the pain.

But more than that? Seeing Deke Marlow lose control to have me had been like an intellectual orgasm. I hadn't cared what he was doing to my body because my mind had reached an altered state where making Deke lose control…validated me, somehow.

His inability to go slow, to make love to me had me believing every word out of his mouth about how desperate he was for me. Even knowing I'd never be as important to him as his friends, his…frantic mating made me feel like I mattered. I was significant to this guy. And for a wallflower, whom no one ever paid attention to, that was an aphrodisiac I was afraid I might be addicted to.

The only time he showed any tenderness at all was after the first time, he had run a hot bath to ease some of the discomfort from his invasion into my body. We sat in his tub with the jets on until our skin started pruning. After that, Deke had taken me to bed again, and repeated everything he had done the first time. He kissed me all over, bringing me another climax before thrusting into me brutally again.

I wish I could say I was offended that he hadn't taken care with my body, and that he ruined my first, second, and third time, but I couldn't say that. His unreasonable need fueled my need to matter to someone. Oh, I knew I

87

mattered to Ava, but she's about the only person who I mattered to on a personal level. I mattered to my parents and the Reynolds as a means to an end.

And as pathetic as it was, the bruising, the bite marks, the hickeys…I reveled in them because, a few days from now, they would be proof that last night really did happen.

"You hungry?"

I looked up and Deke was in the doorway, one shoulder leaning against the frame. I winced as I sat up in Deke's bed, but that couldn't be helped. I hurt all over. "A bit," I replied feeling a bit awkward, which was ridiculous considering this guy has had his face in between my legs.

His head jerked towards the nightstand. "There's a glass of water and some ibuprofen," he said, and I turned my head to see a glass of water and two little tablets. My heart stammered.

I reached over and grabbed the water and pills and downed them in one swallow. I looked back at Deke and asked, "Can…is there time for me to take a shower?"

He stood up straight and walked towards the bed. "It's Saturday," he said casually. "There's time for whatever you want."

Those last words had me wishing I wasn't so sore, which reminded me…"Deke, we need to talk," I said as my stomach hollowed out.

He sat down next to me, and his hand reached out to caress my thigh over the sheets. "Yeah? About what?"

It was hard to concentrate looking into the portrait of such perfection. Deke Marlow was hot as hell. His black hair and green eyes were a lethal combination all their own, but throw in that face and body? No one should be so good-looking.

I finally snapped out of my daze. "We…we didn't use protection last night, Deke," I reminded him. "Not only was that unsafe…it was super reckless. Never mind an STD, a baby would bond us for life." I wish I could say my inexperience made this all Deke's fault, but I couldn't. Yeah, the first time, fell more on his shoulders since he's the one with the experience, but I hadn't protested the next couple of times knowing I was unprotected. I chose pleasure over responsibility and I wasn't going to pretend otherwise.

Deke cocked his head and the edge of his lip lifted as if he was trying not to laugh at me. "Lamb, if you want to get on the pill or something, that's fine," he replied. "However, we're going to keep fucking without protection until you do." He shrugged a shoulder. "If you get pregnant, so be it."

I stared at him dumbfounded.

Absolutely dumbfounded.

He couldn't be serious.

My mind got to working again. "Are you out of your mind?" I whispered, stunned. "Who in the hell wants to be a parent at 18-years-old?"

Deke laughed, further substantiating his insanity. "If it means I get you forever, I'll knock you up every goddamn nine months, Delaney."

I searched his green eyes for signs of alteration, because he had to be on drugs, right? "You...you cannot be serious, Deke," I sputtered. "No one wants to be parents in high school. *No one.*"

He really laughed this time, as if he was privy to some little secret. "I know two guys who would argue that point," he chuckled.

I didn't like being laughed at. I sat up straighter and smoothed the sheet over my lap. "Ramsey and Liam don't count," I flung back.

His brows rose at my tone. "And why don't they count?"

"Because those love stories are legendary, Deke," I pointed out, as if he didn't know.

He smirked. "Ahhhh, I see," he said, his voice dripping with superiority. "Legendary..."

I wanted to smack him again.

"Yes," I huffed. "So, it's okay if Emerson or Roselyn get pregnant because they'll want for nothing for the rest of their lives."

"And you think if I get you pregnant, I'll what?" he asked. "What exactly do you think will happen if I knocked you up?"

Why were we even having this conversation? I *just* freakin' lost my virginity, and Deke was talking about pregnancy like...*holy shit!*

"Do you have *kids?*" I asked incredulously.

Deke's head reared back, and he looked offended. "Fuck no, I don't have any kids," he barked. "Why would you think I have kids?"

Was he for real? "Be...because you're sitting here talking about knocking me up every nine months as if it's no big deal!" I screeched. "You're also talking about teenage pregnancy like it's...normal, or okay."

Deke rolled his eyes, and I seriously wanted to do him bodily harm. "First off, there is nothing wrong with a person if they get pregnant early." He shrugged a shoulder. "Shit happens. Second, we have more money than most. If you or the girls got pregnant, it's not like it would be a struggle."

My eyes felt like they were going to pop out of my head. "We're *teenagers,* for Christ's sake, Deke. We have futures that would be changed forever by a pregnancy."

He shrugged a shoulder again. "All I'm saying is that if *you* don't want to get pregnant, you better work out your birth control soon, because I'm not wrapping it up."

My stomach started churning with an ugly thought. "Do...do you have unprotected sex often?"

I wasn't sure what it was about my question, but Deke looked murderous all of the sudden. "I'm not going to discuss the other girls I've slept with, with you."

"I have the right to know," I hissed, hurt, jealous, and confused. I didn't want to discuss Deke's other conquests any more than he did, but I had the right to know. If he was insisting on having unprotected sex, and I was too weak to stop him, I needed to know.

His mask fell back into place as he said, "I've only had unprotected sex with one other girl in all my life. I can run to the clinic for bloodwork if you're so worried about it, Delaney."

I could swear my heart stopped beating.

Everything that made me a girl wanted his words to have been that, I was the only one, but hearing him admit he's gone bare with one other girl broke my heart. A small part of me wished for the rumor about him and Roselyn to be true because then I'd know, without a doubt, that she'd be the girl he was referring to. If not…well, then that meant there was a girl in Deke's past that he cared enough about to risk his future for.

And then I thought about how I'd feel if it were Roselyn. They were so close, would I feel jealous? Would their friendship make me feel more insecure than I already was?

But then I got to thinking about Roselyn and Liam, and I knew that if Roselyn *was* that girl, whatever they had was long gone. Liam, Roselyn, and Deke wouldn't be as close as they were if there were any residual feelings between Deke and Roselyn.

But I already asked that question, and since Deke wasn't going to tell me anything, I didn't have an answer I could be satisfied with. So, I did my best to seemed grownup and unaffected. "A blood test seems rather ridiculous at this point, don't you think?"

Deke stared at me and, because his poker face was back on, I had no idea what he was thinking. He chucked all conversation when he said, "Go take your shower and meet me in the kitchen for breakfast."

"Then what?"

"Then you spend the rest of the day and night hoping you don't get pregnant," he replied.

CHAPTER 23

Deke ~

I finally allowed Delaney to go home Sunday evening. It was hard, but I had to finally admit that we needed some space. Everything was happening too fast for her, and while I didn't give a fuck, she was unhappy, and I couldn't allow that.

Oh, she spent all weekend letting me pleasure that body of hers, and I introduced her to things that would have had her grandmother clutching her pearls, but Delaney had been unhappy. Even when I was fucking her relentlessly, she hadn't been happy. She had been horny, lustful, aching, and delirious with pleasure, but she hadn't been happy.

She'd been…heartbroken, and I knew it was because I admitted to having bare skin sex with someone else before her. The jacked-up thing? I loved Linnie to pieces, but had I known I would come to feel the way I felt about Delaney, I never would have gone bare with Roselyn. I would have stayed in my lane and let that be for Liam. I was Delaney's only one, but she wasn't mine, and I could see how that would make her feel unimportant.

I had thought about telling her I loved her, but I was afraid she'd think I was only saying it to help pull her out of her insecurities. I wanted Delaney to believe me when I told her.

I also knew I was going to have to talk to Linnie about all this.

We were all posted in front of the school like we usually were, only this time, I was going to let Delaney and Ava walk to first period together. I needed to get my shit together before I approached her. I wanted to be able to tell her about Roselyn.

"Fuck, man," I said, running my fingers through my hair as I watched Delaney and Ava pass us. "How do you guys fucking do it?"

"Do what?" Ramsey asked.

"Let Em and Linnie out of your sights," I replied, frustrated beyond hell.

Liam snorted. "I wouldn't if she didn't live with me," he answered.

"He's right," Ramsey added. "Waking up with Emerson every morning and going to sleep with her every night is the only thing that allows me to let her have a life during the day."

"Move her in, Deke," Liam said. "Move her in this weekend, or you will lose your mind with that unanswered freedom she has." Ramsey grunted in agreement.

We were silent for a bit before I said, "She asked about Roselyn Friday night."

"What did you tell her?" Ramsey asked.

"Nothing," I admitted. "It's not my secret to tell."

Liam's eyes widened, and they looked like huge blue orbs. "You actually told her it was none of her business?"

"No," I huffed. "Well, not in those words, *exactly*. I just told her never to question me about Roselyn ever again." My two best friends were looking at me like I was the dumbest motherfucker on the planet. "What?"

"Deke, how much do you like this girl?" Ramsey asked. I just stared at them, not saying the words. Ramsey let out a deep breath. "That's what I thought."

"You're going to have to tell her, Deke," Liam advised.

"And what about Linnie?" I asked. "We always agreed her reputation would be a priority."

Just then the girls returned from the restroom, and all conversation ceased. It wasn't that any of us were ashamed of the relationship Roselyn had with me and Liam, it just wasn't a topic anymore. Besides, it took a lot of convincing on Liam's part so that Roselyn didn't think badly about herself for what she did, none of us wanted to chance her slipping back into that mind frame.

But I had to talk to her about it.

I needed no secrets between me and Delaney.

The first warning bell rung, and I said, "Linnie, skip first with me, will ya?"

She looked over at Liam. "If I skip with Deke, can I persuade you to share your notes with me?"

Liam's grin was positively wolfish. "I'm positive you can," he replied with a wink.

Emerson laughed while Ramsey just said, "Let's go before we all fucking skip."

As the gang headed towards the school's entrance, I grabbed Linnie's hand and walked her back to my car. We needed absolute privacy for this conversation, and I didn't want to wait until this afternoon when we got out of school. I wanted to settle this...discomfort with Delaney the sooner the better.

Before I lost my ever lovin' mind.

I opened the passenger side door for her, and once she got settled, I closed the door and made my way around the hood to get into the driver's side. When the door shut behind me, she asked, "What's up?"

This was harder than I thought it would be. I was asking Roselyn to give up a piece of herself for someone she didn't even really know. But I had to do it. I was in love with Delaney, and...well, I just had to do it. "Delaney asked me about you Friday night," I told her.

Linnie's bottom lip disappeared between her teeth. After a few seconds, she asked, "About the rumors?"

I nodded. "She asked me if the rumors were true," I admitted.

"What did you say?"

"I told her to never ask me about you again." Linnie's eyes widened. "Then, she asked me if...if I've ever been bare with another girl before."

"With *another* girl?" she stressed. "So, you guys slept together this weekend? It's official?"

I nodded again. "We went to my place after I dragged her out of the party, and she spent all weekend at my place."

Linnie's blue eyes crinkled as she smiled. "Do you love her? Or is it too soon for that?"

I snorted. "Have you met Ramsey and Emerson?" She laughed, but it was time to get serious. "Yes, Linnie," I answered. "I love her-*correction*, I'm in love with her."

Roselyn was quiet for a few seconds before saying, "Let me tell her, Deke."

"Lin-"

She threw her palm up to stop me. "Just hear me out, Deke," she said, and I nodded because...well, this was Roselyn. "No girl wants to know half the story. You can tell her what happened and explain how it's over and all, but she'll have questions about how *I* feel. Hell, she'll have questions about how Liam feels." Roselyn reached over and took my right hand in hers and squeezed. "You can tell her you have no feelings for me other than friendship, but she'll wonder if I have any."

"But-"

"Deke," she continued, interrupting me, "trust me. From someone who...knows, and is a girl, she'll have questions you can't answer. She's going to want to know if...threesomes are something you're into and if she'll need to...accommodate that."

"That's bullshit, Linnie," I barked. "You were the only one and...you were special. *That* wasn't..."

She shook her head but smiled. "I know that, Deke. I've long...gotten over my issues. But...unless you were there, it's hard for people to wrap their minds around what we did. Hell, I *was* there, and I struggled to wrap my mind around it."

"What about Lee?"

Roselyn shrugged a shoulder. "You know he doesn't care about that stuff." She let out a soft laugh. "One thing Liam's made clear is that he's not ashamed of me or what we did. The secrecy was to keep me and Emerson from having to fight them catty bitches that would have come out of the woodwork had they known."

I laughed because she wasn't wrong. Liam and I had never been ashamed of what we shared with Roselyn, but we weren't ignorant of our popularity. We knew if our arrangement got out, Roselyn's life would have been hell. And Emerson's a fighter. She would have been scrapping left and right to defend us.

Looking over at Roselyn, I knew I needed to trust her. "Are you sure this is the way to go?"

"We're the emotional ones, Deke," she answered. "It's better to hear the explanation from someone of the same mindset."

I understood what she was saying, but I didn't necessarily agree with females being the emotional ones, because Delaney made me feel all kinds of emotions. "Okay," I conceded. "We'll do this your way."

"Can I ask you something?" she asked.

"Sure."

"Admittedly, I don't know much about Delaney because we've never run in the same circles, but..." Roselyn gave me a sad smile and I wanted to punch something because I knew what she was going to ask. "Well, do you think she'll-"

"Stop," I growled. "Whatever her opinion of what we did, it will not affect our friendship, Linnie."

"You say that now, bu-"

I shook my head at her. "There's no 'but', Roselyn," I said interrupting her. "If she loves me-"

"Does she?" she cut in sounding hopeful.

I wanted to reassure her, but I couldn't lie. "No," I replied. "Not even a little bit."

CHAPTER 24

Delaney ~

Something was going on.

Deke ignored me this morning as Ava and I walked through the yard into Windsor, and he was quiet during second and third period. He didn't even make me sit with him when he arrived late for second and I was already seated in the front row.

I really started getting anxious when I was able to leave second of my own freewill, meet up with Ava, and go to third without Deke or his entourage present. The only time there was any hint of this weekend was when I had walked into third and Deke was already seated in the back. Our eyes met, and he lifted his chin as if daring me to sit anywhere else.

I wasn't going to lie. I had wanted to sit in the front just to get a reaction out of him because his silence was driving me nuts, but I didn't. I conceded like a wuss and sat next to him, with Roselyn sitting on the other side of him. She had spared me a timid smile, but that was about it. Once third was over, Deke grabbed my hand and walked me to my locker to meet Ava. Once kiss to the side of my head, and he was gone.

I almost cried.

Ava had immediately rushed me to the restroom where we skipped fourth and I told her everything. I hadn't had time to talk to her all weekend other than random texts assuring her I was alive, but Sunday night when I finally got home, I had spent the evening trying to wrap my mind around what I was doing with Deke.

And, now, Ava was staring at me like I just sprouted an extra ear right before her eyes. The scrutiny was making me edgier than I was already feeling. "Quit looking at me like that," I grumbled.

She huffed, "How else am I supposed to look at you, Delaney? I mean...you just told me you spent the entire weekend in bed with Deke freakin' Marlow."

We were sitting on the floor of the last stall with our knees drawn up, our backs against opposite sides. "Oh, come on," I whined. "You knew this was coming. I admitted as much the day he beat up Winston."

Her brows finally found their way back to their original spots. "I know, I know," she muttered. "It's just...holy crap, Delaney. You're sleeping with Deke Marlow."

Holy crap, indeed.

"I know," I whispered miserably. "I just...he's been acting so strange today that...I think the challenge is over, you know."

I saw Ava's beautiful face morph into pure, unadulterated fury. "Delaney, if you're telling me Deke used you this weekend and, now, he's done with you, I will fuck him up, I swear to God," she seethed.

"No, no," I said soothingly. "I don't think it's..." Who was I kidding? I didn't know what anything was like. My eyes started to water, and I think the emotional turmoil of the entire weekend was finally catching up with me. "I...I think I might..."

"Oh, fuck balls," she breathed. "You're in love with him, aren't you?"

I let out a pitiful laugh. "Crash and burn, right?"

She went from outraged to sympathetic instantly. "Where the sharks play," she agreed.

We stayed seated until the lunch bell rang, a sign that fourth period was over. "Since I can't stay in here crying all day, lunch?"

Ava chuckled. "We can always ditch the rest of the day?" she offered.

I shook my head and looked at my best friend. "I'm tired of being a coward," I told her, and I realized I meant that in all things. It was time to face Deke, Winston, my parents, and whoever else felt they had a say in my future.

Ava waited patiently as I splashed my face with some cold water and put myself together. We exited the restroom, but only to be brought up short by Roselyn Bell standing outside the door. She shot Ava a quick glance before looking back at me. "You're a hard girl to find, Delaney," she said sweetly. "This is the fourth place I've looked for you at."

"Why are you looking for me?" I asked. "Is everything okay?"

She glanced at Ava again and said, "Can we...talk privately?"

I looked over at Ava. "It's okay," I assured her. "I'll catch up with you later."

Ava didn't look worried, so much as...sad. Like she was sending me off to meet my doom. "Are you sure?" I nodded before she went on her way.

Roselyn looked towards my back. "Is anyone in there?" she asked referring to the restroom. I shook my head. "Okay, let's go in there." I followed her into the restroom and remained silent as she locked the door, giving us privacy.

When she turned towards me, I asked, "What's this about?" I hadn't meant to sound short, but I wasn't sure how much more my emotions could handle.

Her pretty blue eyes looked serious against her multi-colored hair and easy-going reputation. "Deke, uh...told me about this weekend," she came right out and said. "He told me...you asked him if the rumors were true about me, him, and Liam."

I could feel my face heat with embarrassment. It was one thing to ask Deke when I was calling his bluff on his bullshit, but it was quite another thing to have Roselyn Bell talking to me about this. "I'm...I'm sorry, Roselyn," I muttered. "It wasn't my busin-"

She threw a hand up to stop my apology. "Delaney, it is very much your business since you and Deke are together," she replied.

"Wait, we're no-"

Roselyn held up her hand again to stop my protest. "Whatever you think is going on, Delaney, you and Deke *are* together. You're just...having a harder time coming to terms with it. Trust me, I know."

"How do you know?" I asked, and Roselyn Bell proceeded to tell me about her stepbrother and the night she came to date both Liam and Deke.

I listened in pure fascination as she told me about the suggested gang rape, the way the boys went up to her room to protect her, the way it changed from protection to affection...she told me everything. Well, not details, but the gist of their relationship. The only detail she included was the monogamy, and that's when I knew she was the other girl Deke had referred to.

When she was done with her story, she said, "I'm sorry if...if this makes you uncomfortable or puts a...strain on your relationship with Deke, but I'm not ashamed of the relationship I had with them. And I'm not going to pretend to be, Delaney. It was a secret at the guys' insistence to protect my reputation."

I had so many questions. I mean, I knew people had threesomes, but this hadn't been a threesome. This had been a threesome *relationship*. "Liam doesn't get...jealous?" I asked, putting my confused feelings on hold until I could get a better grasp on this...revelation.

"No," she answered. "It's not like that. Deke was always...extra. It's always been Liam who I connected with and loved. Don't get me wrong. I love Deke to death. He's one of my best friends, but that's it." She looked sad, and worried. "I know it's hard to...understand, but...I wanted to assure you that...other than friendship, there is nothing more between me and Deke, Delaney."

Then a thought occurred to me. "Is that why you and Emerson cleared the air with Ava? Because you guys didn't want to be hypocrites with your relationship with Deke?"

Roselyn smiled, not at all offended by my question. "No," she said, shaking her head. "Emerson was just being Emerson because she's badass like that. I cleared the air because I truly don't think about Liam and Ava. I know firsthand that you can sleep with someone and not be hung up on them afterwards. I know firsthand you can sleep with someone and feel nothing but friendship for them afterwards, Delaney." Her words were hard to digest. "When I look at Deke, I see only my friend-a best friend, but just a friend, nonetheless." She shrugged a shoulder. "I'm just hopeful that when Ava looks at Liam and Ramsey, all she sees is Liam and Ramsey, you know."

"I can tell you that Ava has long moved on since junior high," I assured her. "I...this is just a lot."

Roselyn nodded. "I know," she agreed. "I know, but if things go south between you and Deke, I don't want it to be because of...our past. And I really want us to be friends without...just *real* friends."

It was a lot to take in. I wasn't exactly jealous, but...I was still feeling second best with as loyal as Deke was to her. I knew I needed to take some time to process everything she just told me. Not to mention the way he mostly ignored me all morning had me confused as hell.

"I...it's a lot to take in, Roselyn," I admitted. "And with the way he's been treating me this-"

She huffed out a sweet laugh. "He's acting weird because he thinks you're going to freak out and have nothing to do with him anymore, Delaney," she divulged.

Well..."Oh..."

"Yeah. Oh," she chuckled.

After a few quiet seconds, I said, "Thank you for telling me. I know it couldn't have been easy."

She gave me a short nod. "It is when it's for the right reason," she whispered.

Were Deke and I the right reason?

CHAPTER 25

Deke ~

I was officially a pussy.

I knew Roselyn was talking with Delaney about our past relationship, and my entire body was tense with anxiousness. There was a real possibility that Delaney wouldn't be able to handle our friendship, and I wasn't ready to act on that yet.

Everyone knew where Linnie was and the silence was...morbid. It was like we were all waiting for the knock on the door from a military chaplain to deliver the news. While none of us had known Delaney well, her reputation for being a quiet, sweet wallflower was a huge indicator that she might have issues with what went down between Liam, Linnie, and me. And, sure, she let me do crazy things to her body this weekend, suggesting she was open-minded, but a threesome might be too much for her. Or, at least, a threesome where everyone was still friends afterwards.

Ramsey, Liam, Emerson, and I were seated at our regular lunch table when Ava storming towards us, and there was only one person at this table that she could possibly be pissed at.

Me.

She stopped at the head of the bench, planted her hands flat on the surface, and ignoring everyone else around us, leaned in until her blue eyes were shooting fire directly into mine. "Do you have a minute?" she hissed.

I stood up, waving everyone else to remain seated. They all knew Delaney had spent the weekend with me, but I didn't need our business shouted throughout the entire school eatery. "Lead the way," I said sardonically. I followed Ava through the eatery and out back towards the Ag-Science building. No one ever studied Ag-Science, so it was as quiet as you could get back here.

The second she determined we were clear...

She. Went. Off.

Hands planted on her hips she looked up at me and spewed at me violently. "Look, Deke, I've never had a problem with you before," she started, "but I just spent fourth period with Delaney crying in the fucking school restroom, you sorry sonofabitch! She's crying because you spent all weekend screwing her-which, she's way too fucking good for you to begin with-and this morning you're ignoring her like the hundreds you threw on the nightstand should be good enough!"

I had my hand around her neck and her body slammed up against the wall before she knew what hit her. "Don't you ever fucking talk about Delaney like that again," I hissed in her face.

But Ava didn't back down. Ava was fucking crazy, and I knew it. "Don't ever fucking *treat* Delaney like that again," she hissed back. "I trusted you! I fucking trusted you to take care of her, that's why I called you Friday night. And what do you do? You sleep with her *and* you don't even bother with protection! What the fuck is that? Why…why would you *do* that to her?! Delaney's not some trailer park trash you can fuck with! She's important!"

The only reason I wasn't snapping her fucking neck was because she loved Delaney. She loved Delaney, and she was only doing what I hoped she'd do where Delaney was concerned; protect her. "I'm going to say this, and I'm only going to say it once, Ava," I growled. "This weekend with Delaney is *our* private business-"

"Oh, please," she spewed. "Like your little brood of psychopathic bandits don't already know how you took Delaney's virgi-"

I tightened my hold around Ava's neck, cutting off her next words. "Keep my friends out of this, Ava," I warned. "Don't think that just because I'm in love with Delaney I won't destroy you if you cause problems for *any* of us."

Her eyes almost popped out of her head, and it wasn't because I was depriving her of oxygen. I had accidentally let my feelings for Delaney slip. "Y…" I removed my hand from around her neck, so she could speak. "You're *in love* with Delaney?"

I stood to my full height and looked down at the girl I was going to have to learn to get along with for Delaney's sake. It's not that I really had anything against Ava, it's just I knew she'd always be wary of me and she wasn't necessarily Team Deke.

"This weekend…taking her virginity and possibly getting her pregnant doesn't matter," I answered. "Delaney's mine, and she'll never want for anything for the rest of her life, Ava. She's mine to love, protect, provide for, and cherish. I'm in love with Delaney, and she doesn't have a choice about where we go from here. She's *mine.*"

Ava's face went from furious to…resigned. "Deke, you don't understand," she started to say, "Delaney's special. She's-"

"I know she's special, Ava," I snapped, cutting her off. I knew she didn't think I deserved Delaney, and she was right. But I didn't like hearing it. "She will want for nothing, Ava. *Nothing.*"

She regarded me for a full painful minute before saying, "I don't care about you, Deke. I don't care about you, Ramsey, Emerson, Liam, or Roselyn. I don't care about your...power or your status. If you hurt Delaney...if you betray or hurt her, I will come after you, Deke Marlow. I *will* come after you and I don't care who you have in your corner or who I have to go through to get to you."

I stared down at this girl and I knew she meant every word she just said. She'd go down in burning flames to defend Delaney and it made me wonder just what their relationship was made of. They didn't match, but anyone paying attention could tell they were the real deal.

I took a deep breath and gave Ava a tight nod. "Noted," I grumbled. "But, Ava, I'm not going to hurt her. *Ever.*" Ava gave me a short nod, and I didn't say anything more as she walked away from me.

Returning to the eatery, I spotted Linnie and Delaney sitting at our table. That was good, right? If they were sitting together, then that must mean Delaney was okay with our friendship.

At least, I hoped.

I approached the table and when I got there, instead of sitting where I was when Ava came roaring through, I sat next to Delaney. And I knew it was going to be okay when she quietly dropped her head on my right shoulder in surrender.

I glanced over at Roselyn and she gave me a small smile, but I could see it all in her eyes. Delaney was okay with that part of my life. Now, she might not be okay with everything else going on around us, mainly her parents and Reynolds, but she was okay with what mattered most to me, and that was everyone sitting at this table.

I wasn't worried about Reynolds, because I'd kick his ass every week if I had to in order to get my point across. It was Delaney's parents that I knew would be a problem when I finally faced them. And I would be facing them because there was no way I was going to let Delaney confront them alone. Claiming her meant protecting her, and that meant against anyone, including her parents.

"You okay," I whispered down to her.

I felt her nod against my shoulder. "Yeah, just..."

I brought my face down closer to hers. "Just, what?"

Everyone around us were having their own side conversations, but you could tell there was still some tension at the table. This wasn't like when Ramsey got together with Emerson, or Liam finally claimed Roselyn. We were already connected in some way, shape, or form; Emerson friends with Roselyn, Roselyn involved with me and Liam...

Delaney was new.

She was new to our group, making her an outsider until she committed to me completely. While I was completely committed to her, it was her committing to me that we were all waiting on.

"Just…just don't ignore me again like this morning," she muttered. "That wasn't cool considering…"

I hitched my shoulder, forcing her to lift her head. I reached over, grabbed her, and straddled her across my lap. She gasped but didn't fight me. And since it was just us-the people I trusted-I didn't care if they overheard or not. "I thought you needed some space after this weekend," I told her before admitting, "I needed some space, too."

Her big chocolate eyes looked so serious. "Space from me?"

I shook my head. "No. Space from knowing I was going to have to tell you about Roselyn, sooner or later." She nodded in understanding. "Are you okay with…that?"

"Do I have a choice," she asked, instead of answering.

I shook my head. "No," I told her honestly. "You don't. You don't have a choice in any of this, Delaney, and I'm not going to lie to you and let you believe you do."

She was quiet for a few seconds before asking, "Why?"

I knew what she was really asking, she just didn't want to voice the words for fear of rejection, and I didn't blame her. She's spent her entire life being invisible to everyone who she was supposed to matter to. Ava was her only rock; a girl whose reputation was as horrible as her temper had been her only champion.

"Because I love you," I answered, my voice strong and sure.

"You better," she replied, and I laughed.

I laughed because that's what you do when you're happy.

CHAPTER 26

Delaney ~

The rest of the afternoon had been…weird, but I supposed I should get used to it. Deke and I were officially dating and that meant facing the repercussions of that decision, and that included being friends with his friends, and even though they've all been nice so far, they were still intimidating as hell.

After convincing Deke that I'd head straight for his place after I took care of some stuff after school, he finally let me tend to life, and part of that was standing in front of Winston's house, ringing the bell to his front door.

I waited a few minutes assuming he was here since his car was in the driveway. The front door finally swung open and Winston stood in the doorframe, his face looking better, but still bruised. I wondered, briefly, if he was going to need plastic surgery for his cheekbone.

His eyes widened the second he registered it was me. "Delaney?" His head jerked up and his eyes darted around the yard, presumably looking for Deke. When his eyes met mine again, he asked, "What are you doing here? Is everything okay?"

The sincerity in his voice reminded me of the young boy who used to be my friend. It reminded me of the guy I liked enough to have spent the rest of my life with at one point. "Can we talk?"

His eyes blinking, he shook off his surprise and said, "Yeah, sure. Of course." He stepped back so I could enter his house.

Once I was inside, he shut the door behind him, and the moment wasn't lost on me. I've been in this house a million times growing up. I knew where every room was and how it was decorated. I've sat in the Reynolds' kitchen a gazillion times for luncheons and stuff, but now? I felt so unwelcomed, I wasn't sure which way to step.

"Are your parent home?" I asked, knowing they probably weren't. None of our parents were ever home. This town was so littered with unsupervised children, it was unreal.

He was already shaking his head. "No," he answered. "Last I heard, they were in Japan researching some latest drug and how it affects the pharmaceutical world." He let out a sad laugh. "Well, my dad is. Mom's probably shopping." He jerked his head towards the kitchen. "Want something to drink?"

I nodded my head just for something to do. I felt uncomfortable and...uneasy. Winston's already seen the writing on the wall, but right now I wasn't drunk and emotional. Finally having this conversation sober and alert was going to change his life, too.

I sat down at the kitchen island, placing my purse on the counter as I have many times before, and waited while he grabbed a water from the fridge. He placed it down in front of me, then stepped back until his ass hit the counter. He folded his arms over his chest and said, "Okay, Delaney. Let's get this over with."

Immediately, I felt...guilty. Guilty and sad. It felt as if I was letting everyone down, and I was powerless to stop it, even though that wasn't true. All I had to do was walk away from Deke Marlow and life would go on as per usual for Winston, my parents, and the Reynolds.

But I couldn't.

I knew I couldn't long ago, but I definitely knew I couldn't after Deke told me he loved me.

"I'm not drunk now," I said, stating the obvious.

"No. You're not," Winston whispered in agreement.

"I'm sorry, Winston," I said dismally. "I never meant for any of this to happen."

His arms dropped, and I saw his hands grip the counter lip behind him. "We're not supposed to be married for another four years, Delaney," he reminded me. "Why...why do this? Do you seriously see yourself with Deke Marlow for the next fifty years?"

No, I didn't.

Teenage love is just that; teenage love. People in love always think it's going to be forever. I mean, people don't fall in love thinking it's going to end someday. But I wasn't one of those people. Deke said he loved me, but there's carefree teenage love and then there's adult going-through-hard-times love. I believed that Deke loved me right now, but a year from now? When all the novelty wears off?

I shook my head. "No, Winston," I answered. "I don't see myself with Deke in fifty years, but that doesn't change how I feel." I let out a deep breath. "We're friends. We've known each other most our lives. And...and that was enough for me to stick to the agreement. I wasn't look for..."

"Passion?" he supplied.

I gave him a tight nod. "Yeah. Passion." *God, this sucked.* "And now that I know what that feels like...well, I'm not willing to settle anymore."

"We can try t-"

I threw my hand up to stop him. "We did that once already, Winston. We *both* were left wanting," I reminded him.

Winston stared at me for several painfully uncomfortable seconds before asking, "And what about our parents? What am I supposed to tell them?"

"I'll handle my parents," I said. "You...tell them the truth. I fell in love with someone and-"

"*What?!*" he snapped. "What the fuck do you mean you *fell in love* with someone? You've known Deke Marlow a fucking week, Delaney. A *week* and you're talking *love?* Are you insane?"

I could barely get the words out of my mouth. "So what, if it's only been a week?" I said through clenched teeth. "You don't know how I feel."

Winston let out a dark laugh. "Fuck, you girls," he swore. "You chicks always think it's love when you get dick for the first time." There was no way he could know that I slept with Deke, but his next words stopped my thoughts. "And don't sit there and try to tell me you haven't fucked him already, Delaney. Deke Marlow isn't the type of guy who goes around holding hands on chaperoned dates. And there's no way you'd be throwing away our future if you hadn't ridden his dick already."

"Quit being an asshole," I clipped out.

His brows rose. "Ah, but I see you're not denying it," he accused.

I stood up. "How can you be...angry?" I almost said jealous, but that didn't sound right. "You've slept with dozens of girls, Winston. Why are you so bothered by who I'm sleeping with?"

"Because you're throwing away our future!" he roared, finally losing grip on his composure. "I may have fucked my fair share of females, Delaney, but I *never* jeopardized our futures!"

"You can find someone else to further your parents' agenda, Winston," I pointed out. "It doesn't have to be me!"

And the truth came out like a right hook to my ribs. "But you're the only one who would have stayed in the background and taken it!" he yelled.

My lungs lost their ability to breathe. Even though I knew what my future with Winston would have entailed, hearing him admit it was like a slap in the face. It showed me we weren't even friends at this point. Friends didn't humiliate each other. He would have cheated, but more importantly, he wouldn't have tried to hide it. My dignity wasn't worth the effort.

He must have realized what he just admitted because his head dropped, and I could see him taking a deep breath to steady himself. "You're a bastard," I hissed. "You're a selfish bastard just like our fathers."

Winston's head shot up and he speared me with a look so hateful, I was thankful to be on the other side of the island. "I am *nothing* like those two assholes," he seethed.

I stared at the boy who was once my friend, and I knew that, even if I wanted to forgive his careless words, my life was moving in a different direction, with or without Deke Marlow. I was no longer the same Delaney Martin I was two weeks ago.

"I'm going to call my parents tonight and let them know there will no longer be a marriage after college," I informed him.

Winston lifted a brow. "Deke Marlow's going to break your heart, Delaney," he said coldly. "He's going to ruin your ability to love along with the secured future you had with me."

He still didn't understand. This wasn't about Deke. This was about me. *I* was different, no matter the outcome with Deke. "Be that as it may, Winston, it doesn't change anything."

The corner of his lips lifted, and it wasn't in a smile. It was a sneer. "When he's done with you? When he finally gets bored and moves on to someone…more his class? I'll be here waiting for you."

It was the final slap in the face. He was implying that he's more than willing to wait because he knows it's going to happen. "Winston it's over no matter how things play out between me and Deke," I repeated. "It's over."

He cocked his head as he said, "You know your way out, Delaney." It was cold and…mean.

I grabbed my purse, hooked it over my shoulder and said, "Goodbye, Winston," as I turned my back on him and walked out the Reynolds' home.

It wasn't until I was sitting in my car that I felt I could finally breathe. Now, I had to call my parents and tell them, and they were going to be harder to deal with than Winston. Never having gone up against my parents before, I wasn't too proud to admit that I needed Deke with me to do this. I needed a physical, visual reminder of why I was doing this.

I needed his strength.

CHAPTER 27

Deke ~

I knew Delaney had gone to Reynolds' house, and it had taken everything in me to let her-to trust her. Now, it wasn't that I didn't trust Delaney, per se. It's just I've never been in love before and it's a fucked-up feeling, if I was being honest.

It's the lack of control I was struggling with, and with eyes finally wide open, I was understanding Ramsey and Liam more, and more now. I used to think they were unhinged with the way they stressed out whenever the girls weren't around, but I got it now.

Boy, did I fucking get it.

The rest of the school day had gone fine, and by the time the end of the day rolled around, it was all over the school that Delaney Martin was my girlfriend. *Mine.* There was no more confusion or love triangle with Reynolds. So when Delaney told me she was going to his house after school so they could talk, a part of me knew it was the right thing to do, but the rest of me wanted to conk her on the head and never let her leave my cave.

Finishing up in the gym, I heard the doorbell ring, and I prayed it was Delaney. I'd been working out for two hours trying to occupy my time, so I didn't storm over to Reynolds' place and drag her home, and I was barely hanging on.

Wearing only my basketball shorts, I opened the door to a forlorn-looking Delaney. "Hey, baby," I said, stepping back and letting her in, noticing she didn't have an overnight bag.

Fuck.

"Hey," she returned walking towards the living room and sitting down.

I sat down on the coffee table across from her. "I take it things didn't go well?" I prompted.

Delaney shrugged a shoulder. "It's not that it went…bad," she hedged. "It was just a bit, sort of…uncomfortable."

Oh, I bet it was. "Did he get pissed?" Any excuse. *Any* excuse to fuck him up again.

Her beautiful face looked absolutely miserable. "He got…resentful," she muttered.

Resentful?

I was going to fuck him up.

"Meaning?" I said, prompting her to say more.

"Ugh," she groaned, and threw her head back rather dramatically. When her eyes met mine again, she said, "He basically said that we don't have to decide anything for another four years, and…"

I couldn't stop my hands from clenching into matching fists. "And, what?"

Her eyes narrowed as she regarded me. "Promise you won't go off half-cocked?"

Wow.

That was encouraging.

"Delaney…" I growled.

"Promise me, Deke," she ordered, rather sternly.

"Do not confuse my love for you for a weak spine, Delaney," I advised. "You will *not* lead me around by my dick just because I love you, understand that."

She looked taken aback by my comments. "Are you for real?" she screeched. "You are equating me asking you not to get upset to leading you around by your dick? That's absurd, Deke!"

My problem was that I was new to this. I was feeling weak, unsure, and irritated primarily because, while I've already told Delaney how I feel, she's yet to tell me. I could have pushed it at school, but I didn't want to. I needed Delaney *willingly* goddamn it, and the wait was killing me.

"What the fuck did Reynolds say?" I demanded.

Delaney stood up and started pacing the room. "Unbelievable," she muttered to herself.

"Delaney, if you don't want me going over there and beating it out of him, tell me!" I thundered.

She whirled around on me pissed. "He said he'll be waiting when you get tired of me!" she yelled back. "Are you happy?!"

The rage I was feeling was real. "And when you told him I wouldn't because I was in love with you?"

Her anger dissipated instantly. Her shoulders drooped and her eyes averted mine. "Uhm…"

I had her arms in my hands and her back up against the wall before she could utter another word. "So help me God, Delaney, you better have told him we're in love and that's why you're putting an end to that ridiculous agreement," I seethed, pissed beyond what I ever thought I could be.

She looked up at me and mumbled, "It seemed…that's private."

Private my motherfucking ass.

"You didn't tell him because you believe him, don't you?" I snarled. "You think I'm going to drop you and I'm just bullshitting you, don't you? You're embarrassed to tell him I love you because you think it makes you look stupid."

Her eyes started to shine. "Deke..." she mouthed. When she said I'd better love her, she wasn't being cute or flirty; she meant that shit.

My hands tightened around her arms, sure to leave bruises, and I shook her enough to get her undivided attention. "I need you to pay attention, Delaney," I spat. "I need you to pay really good attention, right now. I love you. I fucking *love* you. I've never said those words to another girl in all my motherfucking *life*." Her eyes widened, and her face looked stunned. "And, while it would be nice, I don't frankly give a fuck if you love me back or not, because you're mine, *regardless*." I pushed up her against the wall one more time to emphasize my point. "I'm never going to let you leave me, Lamb. *Ever.*"

Her eyes blinked one time.

One. Time.

One time before her hands were attacking the waistband of my shorts. "Delaney, bab-"

"Shut up," she snapped as she pushed my shorts down.

"I'm all sweaty, baby," I pointed out at the same time I was releasing my hold on her. In the time it took for her to kick off her sandals, unbutton her jeans, push them down along with her panties, and jump into my arms, my dick was rock hard and ready.

With her arms wrapped around my neck and her legs wrapped around my waist, she panted, "I don't care, Deke. Fuck me, please."

And, so, I did.

I plowed my cock deep into her pussy with one thrust. She screamed, and I groaned, it felt so good.

She felt so good.

But I was done waiting. I drove into her so hard, her back was slamming into the wall behind her. "Tell me," I demanded. "Fucking tell me before I lose my fucking mind, Lamb."

"Harder, Deke," she begged. "Fuck me harder."

Christ. "That's not what I'm asking, and you fucking know it," I barked.

Delaney started bouncing up and down on my cock, trying to impale herself when she finally said it. "I love you, Deke," she panted. "I...I love you, even if I shouldn't."

I let that last part slide because she finally told me what I wanted to hear, and the rest didn't matter. My insecurities, her insecurities-they didn't matter right now. All that mattered was that Delaney was mine. I was going to spend every night inside her body, one way or another, and no one would ever be able to take her from me.

"Tell me how badly you want my cock, baby?" I grunted. "Tell me how you're mine."

Delaney was withering and moaning. "I can't…think, Deke…"

Music to my ears.

I kept slamming into her, our harsh breathing the only sounds in the house, and I didn't want it to ever end. Her pussy wrapped around my dick was a high more pure than anything out there. Delaney Martin was more potent than any drug I have ever tried.

"Don't stop, Deke," she whimpered. "I'm…I'm going to cum…"

My dick throbbed with my need for release as I slammed Delaney harder against the wall. "That's it, baby," I encouraged her. "Give it to me. Soak my dick with your cream, Lamb."

Delaney threw her head back and cried out as her pussy gripped my dick in a choke hold and started convulsing all around me. *"Deke!"*

I followed immediately after. *"Delaney…"* I hissed into her neck right before biting down. My previous mark had started to fade, and I didn't like it.

After a few exhausting seconds, we both slid to the floor, where she draped her body over mine, straddling my now soft cock. "Jesus Christ," she muttered.

My hands rested on her hips as I stared at the ceiling. "I'm not going to drop you, Delaney," I said, hoping she'd believe me, eventually.

She let out a deep breath before saying, "Even if you do, Deke, I'm past…whatever I wanted in life before you. Winston and our parents are just going to have to accept that."

I didn't comment, but I knew we were going to have to have a serious talk about what it meant to be in a relationship with me before I strangled her to death.

CHAPTER 28

Delaney ~

Deke spent the rest of the night using my body and professing his undying love for me.

Okay.

Maybe not *quite* like that, but I'm guessing the constant 'you're mine's were relative to the same thing as professing one's undying love.

I did learn, however, that what we did Friday night was nothing compared to how we spent last night. It was almost as if, now that I wasn't a virgin any longer, Deke didn't have to hold back.

I also learned just how dark Deke's desires could scale. He liked rough sex, and he liked dirty sex and, after last night, a blushing wallflower I no longer was.

Deke liked control, and not just your average everyday role identifications as me being the woman and him being the man. No. Deke liked sinister control. The kind of control where you had to trust the person entirely; where you had to trust that it was still consensual sex.

Deke had spent all night holding me down and making me take whatever he had to give me, and it had taken some serious getting used to. He also liked to talk dirty, and the language coming from his lips had been another acclimation I had to get used to.

But after every time he held me close and just...*held me.*

It was as if letting him to whatever he wanted to my body was some sort of validation or something. Like...he was trying to scare me off, but it wasn't working, so he felt...better. I don't know. It's weird to experience, much less try to explain.

He had also made it clear that I needed to start bringing a change of clothes to his house because I was going to need it. I think he was half-ass moving me into his house with him. But, until then, I was back at my house getting ready for school.

I had time for a bite to eat before school, but my phone rang as I dropped two slices of bread into the toaster. It's weird, the house staff did their thing during school hours, so I rarely saw them, but I always had pre-made dinners in the fridge to eat. Breakfast wasn't included, so toast it was. Pulling my phone out of my pocket, I saw it was my mother, and I couldn't stop the groan even if I had wanted to.

"Good Morning, Mother," I answered.

"Delaney Martin," she snapped, and I already knew, "what is this nonsense I'm hearing from the Reynolds that you've…you've terminated the agreement between our families?"

Jesus. This really was a business transaction.

"I was going to call-"

"Delaney, what are you thinking?" she asked, not caring about interrupting me.

"Mom-"

"I mean…this…this is our future," she sputtered.

"*Our* future?"

"I meant yours, of course," she bit back, correcting her slip of the tongue.

Little did she know, that gave me the perfect opening. "And as it's my future, I decided I want something different, Mom," I replied. "I'm not happy with the idea of marrying Winston just to secure a solid financial foundation for you and the Reynolds. I want to be happy."

"Nonsense, Delaney," she clipped. "You'll be perfectly happy with Winston-"

I let out a sigh. "No, I won't, Mother," I said, this time cutting her off. "I met a guy and-"

She scoffed. "Delaney, please. I've heard all about the boy you're throwing Winston over for. The Reynolds told me everything."

"You got an opinion about a guy from the people who stand to lose just as much as you do, and you believe them? Seriously?"

"What about Blaineview?" she asked, ignoring my question. "You know they'll take you on because of your grades and being our only child. You're not throwing that away, also, are you?"

I had never wanted to go to Blaineview. I wanted to go to Dartmouth. I wanted to go to an East Coast school to get as far away from my stifling future as I could. My parents thought I needed to go to college with Winston. It was assumed he'd attend Blaineview like a majority of Windsor graduates, but he's mentioned over the years wanting to explore his options.

"We've talked about this, Mom. I want to go to Dartmouth," I reminded her.

"And we talked about how it's more beneficial to follow Winston," she reminded *me.*

"But Winton's a nonfactor now, Mother," I volleyed back.

She was silent for a while and that meant Mrs. Shirley Martin was reassessing her approach. My mother might seem like a vapid socialite, but she was more cunning than people gave her credit for. The scar on my face is proof enough of that.

"How about we make you a deal, Delaney," she posed. "We'll set up a tour at Dartmouth this weekend for you, but you have to...consider Winston a bit more."

"Mom-"

"Hear me out, Delaney," she implored. "Four years is a long time, don't you agree?"

I glanced at my watch that showed four *minutes* was a long time. "Yes," I agreed, nevertheless.

"High school romances have a tendency to fizzle out, and...and I'm not saying that in an unsupportive way." I almost snorted. "I'm saying that as a matter of fact, Delaney."

The jacked-up part?

She wasn't lying.

It was very rare for high school sweethearts to make it through the grownup stages in life together. People grow up and change. What you want at thirty is a far cry from what you wanted at sixteen. There were no guarantees, and even if Deke and I gave it our all, we could still eventually drift apart later down the line.

Four years was a long time, and anything could happen. Hell, I had been using that same argument every time I defended my arrangement to Ava. I lost count of how many times I've said Winston could end up meeting someone in college and falling in true love. If I went to Dartmouth and Deke went to Blaineview, the same thing could happen to either one of us. I mean, hell...how many times has a person thought themselves in love only to find real true love later in life and realized every relationship beforehand hadn't compared?

I knew I was in love with Deke, but just like he said his love for me didn't make him weak, I couldn't let my love for him make me stupid.

So, I agreed.

I agreed that I shouldn't be so closed minded to all of life's possibility for something so brand new and unchartered.

"Okay, Mom," I conceded. "I won't...take Winston off the table completely, just yet, but you have to promise to give Deke a chance. Even if...things don't work out with me and Deke, he still deserves a fair chance. It's not his fault I've changed my mind."

"Why...why don't we concentrate on college right now, since that's the next step your life, and we'll deal with everything else as it comes?" she suggested.

I wanted to argue and...*make* her acknowledge my relationship with Deke, but I knew I had a better chance of making her see things my way face to face. I should probably be grateful that she bothered to call and discuss this, at all. Her or my father could have easily cut off all my finances and gone the bullying and intimidation route.

"Sounds good, Mom," I lied. "I'll...I'll talk to you later."

"Of course, dear," she replied smoothly. "I'll set up your tour and email you all the information later today."

"Okay," I muttered. "I need to go, Mom. I'm going to be late for school."

The smile in her voice told me she thought she won this round, and I suppose she did. "Oh, certainly, honey. Talk to you later."

"Bye, Mom." I hung up not waiting for her to say bye back, and I felt absolute retched.

I felt...the entire conversation felt like...betrayal of some sort. Even though I knew I was done with Winston, just agreeing with my mother made me feel...underhanded.

The toast had popped up out of the toaster long ago and was already cold, so I threw the two slices in the trash and hoped Ava had her ever stash of granola bars in her bag. The crazy girl said she always had granola bars because you never knew if kidnappers were lurking about or not, and you needed food to survive after escaping their sex trafficking ring. I gave her the kidnapping, because...well, we were the children of the One-Percent, but sex trafficking? Kidnapping for ransom was more likely.

With my sore body exiting my house and getting into my car, I wondered what I was going to tell Deke. I've never had to answer to anyone before or take someone else into consideration when I went somewhere or did something, so it felt weird.

But...Deke couldn't get upset with a college tour, right?

I mean...right?

CHAPTER 29

Deke ~

I let Delaney go on that stupid weekend tour to Dartmouth because I was in love with her, and I was quickly realizing that love equated to stupidity on a grand fucking scale.

She had sounded so excited when she told me Tuesday that her parents had set up a tour for her at Dartmouth, I hadn't had the heart to tell her she was already enrolled in Blaineview, and she'd be going to school with us. I had also made a mental note to find out what Ava's college plans were. If we could get her to go to Blaineview with us, I knew Delaney would feel much better about going.

Another reason I let her go was because she said her parents were meeting her at Dartmouth and she wanted to use this opportunity to talk to them face to face about our relationship. She had told me all about the conversation she had with her mother Tuesday morning, and her mother sounded like a real piece of manipulative work.

The fucked-up thing was that I didn't care if Delaney's parents liked me or not. Their opinions had no impact on Delaney's future with me. I just wanted her universally happy, if possible. I knew it was going to be a hard sell because any parents willing to physically harm their child for the sake of money had to be evil. I had no doubt they would fight tooth and nail to convince her to still marry Reynolds, but it wasn't going to happen. I just had to stay back until she called on me to help.

It's one of the hardest things I've ever had to do.

"Uh…Deke," Emerson's voice broke through my thoughts, but it was more her tone.

We were all at Ramsey's getting ready to spend the day at the cove for another day party with a barbeque and all that shit. The only person missing was Delaney as I'm sure Ava would be in attendance.

With everyone in the kitchen grabbing drinks and shit, I turned towards

Emerson. Roselyn was standing next to her and they were both looking at something on her phone. "Yeah?"

I watched the girls share a look before Emerson's silver eyes landed on mine. "Uhm...did you say Delaney was meeting her parents for her tour of Dartmouth?" I nodded. "*Just* her parents?"

Before I could answer, Linnie breathed out, "Oh, shit."

I was at their side, plucking Emerson's phone out of her hand before they knew it, and there on the screen, was a picture of Delaney, Winston, and their parents with the caption reading 'New school. New Beginnings. New Family. Congratulations, Delaney & Winston!' It had been posted to social media and somehow landed on Emerson's notifications.

No fucking way.

"Now, Deke," Linnie said softly, like a trainer approaching a wounded tiger at the zoo, "we have no idea-"

My eyes shot towards her. "She said she was going *alone*, Roselyn," I bit out. "She said she was going alone and meeting her parents there. She didn't say fuck all about Reynolds and his parents."

"Deke," Emerson joined in, "for all we know, she did. Her parents could have ambushed her, you know."

After that disaster between Ramsey and Emerson when Ramsey had jumped to conclusions without letting Emerson explain, I knew she was just trying to give Delaney the benefit of the doubt, but that picture didn't display a girl who was upset about being ambushed.

"Emerson, look at the fucking picture!" I spewed, Ramsey taking his rightful place behind her by the time I was done hissing at her. She took her phone back, studied the photo, and just bit her lip, saying nothing.

She knew I was right.

"Maybe you should call her and-"

I cut Roselyn off. "Fuck that, Linnie," I snapped. "Even if she was ambushed, she should have called me and told me. Or, better yet, gotten the fuck out of there. It's not like she's broke and can't afford a motherfucking plane ticket!"

I had never been so livid in all my life. They must have gotten to her. She showed up and her parents had the Reynolds in tow and convinced Delaney how perfect their lives could all still be. They probably spent all day reminding her of the *good times*. And because Delaney's always been...pliable, she probably caved within an hour.

Never mind that she's spent every night with me this week. Never mind that I've fucked her a million different ways, cumming inside her with no thought to the consequences. Sure, she ended up getting the shot Monday afternoon, but that didn't mean shit. The dice had already been thrown.

"Deke, you need to call her," this from Liam. "Yeah, the picture looks bad, but...there could be a very innocent reason for it."

I scanned the faces of my friends, and knowing they were only trying to help, I gave in. I yanked my phone from my back pocket and dialed Delaney. I dialed Delaney and motherfucking Winston Reynolds answered her phone, "Deke."

"Where the fuck is Delaney, Reynolds?" I growled into the phone.

"She's in the middle of her tour," he answered. "Look, Deke, don't make this…situation harder than it needs to be."

Winston Reynold's was a dead man.

"Meaning?"

"Delaney belongs with me, Deke," he said, believing he was safe over the phone. "I admit I dropped the ball by taking her for granted, and I'll have to live with that. I'll have to live with the fact that you…will always matter in her life. But she's always belonged with me. Our families…well, you can't undo years of friendship."

I clenched the phone so tightly, it's a wonder it didn't crack in my hand. "You're with her in New Hampshire?"

"Check social media," he taunted. "That should tell you everything you need to know."

I had to steady myself. Rage was threatening to shatter my psyche. I wanted to kill Reynolds for daring to come between me and Delaney, and I wanted to kill Delaney for being so weak; so spineless.

She said she loved me, but she'd rather be with Winston because it was easier than standing up to her parents. Even though she had me to fight alongside with her, she was too weak to see it through.

I told Delaney I would never let her go, but that was when I thought she wanted me just as badly as I did her. That's when I thought she loved me more than she loved simplicity. And, truth be told, no one that weak belonged in our group.

"You can have Delaney, Winston," I hissed into the phone, pretending that rage wasn't corroding my soul. "But a word to the wise…you better stay away from me, and you sure as fuck better keep Delaney away from me, or I will ruin the rest of your lives, Reynolds. I will spend every resource I have making you jump to your own deaths if either of you come within spitting distance of me."

He was quiet for a few seconds before saying the words that guaranteed we'd be meeting up really soon, "It won't matter because, in the end, I'll have Delaney." I hung up the phone and threw it across the kitchen, not caring when it shattered against the wall.

"Deke…" Emerson whispered.

I didn't look at her.

I didn't look at anyone.

I didn't look at anyone or utter a word as I heard Ramsey say, "Hey, baby, why don't you and Roselyn go to the party without-"

"You're out of your goddamn mind if you think I'm leaving Deke like this," she snapped. "I'm not going *anywhere,* Reed." Ramsey let out a sigh because, like we all knew, whenever Emerson called him Reed, we knew she was serious.

"I'm not leaving either," Roselyn piped up.

"Okay," Liam said. "Just…you girls go watch a movie…or something, while…uhm, we take care of this."

I could hear the girls shuffle out of the kitchen and it wasn't until I was certain they were out of earshot that I looked up at Liam and Ramsey. With their girls gone, they let their feelings show plainly on their faces.

They were just as livid as I was.

"Who do you want to destroy first?" Ramsey asked.

That was easy.

Delaney.

Reynolds isn't the one who was tearing a patch in my chest.

"I'll handle Delaney," I replied, cold and…just fucking *cold*. "You can take her parents and Liam can take the Reynolds."

"And Winston?" Liam asked.

"I'll handle him when I'm done with Delaney," I promised. "Their blissful future is going to be her feeding him through a straw for the rest of their lives."

CHAPTER 30

Delaney ~

I was so irritated, it wasn't even funny. Not only had this tour turned out to be nothing like I had imagined, I lost my phone, and I missed Deke.

Visiting Dartmouth had been a big eye opener to how much I didn't want to be on the East Coast while Deke was at Blaineview on the West Coast.

But more irritating than anything else had been when we had all gone out to dinner after the tour was over and the Reynolds had joined us. My parents tried to play it off as a happy coincidence, but I knew better. I also started to question the loss of my phone. Had I had it on me, I would have called an Uber, gone to the airport, and bought a ticket home.

Now, it was late evening, and I was at the store, buying a new phone. Sure, the sales associate was kind enough to activate my backup and all my apps, but it was still a pain in the ass. Not to mention, my parents were having after dinner cocktails with the Reynolds and they were seriously expecting me to show up and play polite. And, once upon a time, I might have-but not anymore.

Knowing Deke had my back, and was waiting at home to slay dragons for me, gave me a sense of strength I never knew I possessed. Sure, I wasn't a complete pushover, but I never viewed myself as strong as Ava, as brave as Roselyn, or as badass as Emerson.

But being with Deke made me feel all those things.

I knew I had been played by my parents, but I was actually grateful for the experience because I knew now, without a doubt, I wanted to be with Deke wherever he went.

The second the sales associate finished setting up my phone, it started chiming uncontrollably with notifications, missed calls, and message alerts.

The first notification I saw was Ava's text message begging me to call her ASAP, so I did. "Ava?"

"Oh, my God, Delaney," she cried breathlessly. "Where are you?"

"I'm still in New Hampshire," I told her. "I lost my phone and had to buy a new one. I just walked out of the store and I was about to order an Uber back to the hotel, but your text was urgent."

"So, you haven't been online at all today?"

"No," I answered, suddenly nervous. "Even if I hadn't lost my phone, I wouldn't have answered it during the tour. That would have been rude."

I could hear Ava taking a deep breath over the phone, and the hairs on the back of my neck stood up. "Delaney," she whispered desperately, "there's a picture of you and Winston with both your parents at Dartmouth with a caption about new beginnings or something like that."

I could feel my lungs tighten up with the unbelievability of her words. "Ava," I breathed, "Winston and his parents are here, that's true, but there's no picture. We didn't take any pictures together."

"Delaney, what the hell are you doing there with Winston and his parents?" she asked incredulously.

"I'm not here with them," I stressed. "My parents ambushed me, trying to change my mind about marrying Winston. But there's no-"

"Delaney, pull up your social media feed," she said, interrupting. "There's a picture."

I quickly did what she suggested, and sure as shit, staring up at me was the picture we all took last year when we had all taken a trip to New York. I had mentioned wanting to go to Dartmouth back then, and to humor me, we'd gone to the campus and taken a group selfie.

Scrambling to get back on the phone, I said, "Ava, that's the picture from last year when we'd all gone to New York."

"Well, Winston posted it making it look like it's from today," she said sadly.

"Fuck..." I muttered.

"Delaney, you need to call Deke, and you need to call him *now*," she groaned. "He's going to be pissed, chic."

"I have my purse on me," I said. "Every...everything else at the hotel can stay. It's just clothes and stuff. I'm heading to the airport. I'm flying home now, okay."

"Text me when you're getting ready to land, and I'll pick you up," she offered.

I did the math; it was only 7pm here, so it was only 4pm in California. If I could get a direct flight, I could be in California by nine, maybe ten. The hour drive to Sands Cove would land me at home no later than eleven. It was a Saturday night, so Deke was sure to still be up that late. I could get to him and explain how the picture was from last year.

"Okay," I told her. "Let me get an Uber and I'll text you with my flight information once I get a ticket."

"Be careful, Delaney," she replied. "Be careful but get here before Deke does something stupid."

"Yeah, okay," I said before hanging up and ordering an Uber.

As soon as the car pulled up, and I confirmed it was my driver, I directed him towards the nearest airport. In the backseat, I dialed Deke, and when he didn't answer, I dialed him again. After the fourth time of him not answering, I sent him a text. I waited, and waited, but he never responded or called back.

When I got to the airport, I had to put Deke on hold to get my ticket. And because The Lord was on my side, I managed to get a direct flight off a cancellation. It costs me-or rather, my parents-an arm and leg, but I didn't care. I was feeling…uneasy, and I needed to get home.

I texted Ava my flight information, and after one last attempt to get a hold of Deke, I stowed away my phone and boarded my flight. To avoid being on the news as a missing persons or a runaway, I had sent off a quick text to my parents to let them know I caught a flight home. I wasn't sure if they'd even see it, but I didn't care. I knew, now, that they set me up and stole my phone. They wanted to make sure I wouldn't see what Winston posted. They wanted to make sure it was up long enough to ruin me and Deke.

But the joke was on them. This wouldn't ruin anything between me and Deke because…well, we were in love. People in love don't choose the words and actions of others without listening to their partner first, right?

Sure, that picture looked bad, but once I pull it up on my social media account and show him the first time it was posted, he'd see the manipulation tactic for what it was, right?

Right???

Once we were up in the air, I called Deke again, but this time when he didn't answer, I left a message. I explained that, while the picture was real, it had been taken last year. I rambled on so much, the voicemail cut me off.

The problem was that this was all my fault, and I knew it.

It was my fault for still harboring that deep-seated need to believe that my parents aren't the same people who held me down and scarred my face for profit. While the latchkey kids of Sands Cove were used to absent parents, it didn't necessarily mean we *liked* it that way. We were *used* to it, but that didn't mean we were unfeeling and didn't want loving parents.

When my mother had agreed to a compromise, I knew deep down she was up to something, but the hopeful part of me convinced myself that her offer had been genuine. I knew better, but I went anyway. Deep down, I knew better, and I had to take responsibility for that.

Sitting on the plane, I knew my life before I boarded was over. My parents would end up resorting to blackmail, and I knew I'd have to walk away with nothing to my name. After all, I was a legal adult. They were no longer obligated to care for me if I didn't want to play by their rules.

I thought about my bank account and how it was a joint account with their names on it. I was going to have to go into town and withdrawal as much as I could in the morning. Luckily for us, the financial foundation of Sands Cove was prominent enough that we had banks that were opened during the weekend.

Also, lucky for me, because my parents didn't want to deal with me, I was authorized to withdrawal as much as wanted. I was going to have to hit the bank first thing and buy a car next. The car I had now was in my parents' names because they paid for the insurance.

Holy Christ...I was going to have to find a job!

I knew, even if Deke was upset with me, Ava would let me stay with her until I figured things out, but I was hoping it wouldn't come to that. I had hundreds of thousands in my bank account, and while I couldn't afford a house like I have now, I could easily afford a condo or something small in town. Sands Cove had a working-class population just like every other town in the world, and the people who made this town possible lived affordably in town. I could do that, too.

I didn't need...extra.

I glanced at my phone and still saw nothing from Deke. The part that loved him hoped he was just partying and not checking his phone thinking I was busy in New Hampshire with my parents. The part that loved him was hoping he was playing basketball with Ramsey and Liam. The part that loved him was hoping he was in an online battle with Ramsey and Liam for zombie domination.

But the part of my brain that trumped love with logic told me he was avoiding my calls and messages. Common sense told me there was no way Deke could avoid his phone or social media long enough not to have seen the picture or see my texts.

Common sense told me I was in deep shit.

CHAPTER 31

Deke ~

Delaney was texting and calling so much that I finally turned my phone off. I didn't need it on anyway, since the only people who I gave a fuck about were here with me.

After Ramsey, Liam, and I discussed the details of how we'd handle our *assignments*, we convinced the girls I wasn't psychotic, and we all headed out to the day party at the cove. The girls hadn't really been on board, but what could they do? Wanting to make sure none of us ended up in prison, they had to follow.

We had arrived around six o'clock because we had convened in Ramsey's study and did our research into the Reynolds and the Martins. It had taken longer than I had anticipated, but by the time we were done, we had everything we needed to ruin their lives as they knew it.

Their debts and finances had been easy, but Ramsey had been able to dig up some dirt on Winston's father. Apparently, he's not as heterosexual as he pretended to be. And, while there was nothing wrong with being gay, there was when you were married to a woman and you were cheating on her with twinks during your random travels.

Winston had nothing on him other than he fucked anything that moved, but that didn't matter. Delaney knew he fucked around, and she really hadn't cared. Anything else he did was no worse than what the rest of us did, so he was a dead end.

His mother had no skeletons, and from what we could gather on her, she was just stupid. She spent all her time shopping and…shopping.

As for Delaney's parents, we were able to find out her father was in debt, and not your average household debt, but in *real* debt. While they were wealthy, wealth is relative when you're placing half a million dollar bets on red. They were living on borrowed money, and he needed Delaney to marry Winston to secure his medical research and partner with Winston's father's pharmaceutical empire.

Delaney's mother was also screwing some dude who lived in Monte Carlo. Her dad used Monte Carlo as a cover for research when he was really gambling. And he didn't care where his wife ran off to because he was too busy giving into the monster in his mind. Delaney's mother didn't mind the gambling because she was too busy spreading her legs for a guy half her age.

All the while, they were going broke, and Delaney was none the wiser.

As for Delaney, of course, there was nothing on her. No vices, no speeding tickets, not even a fucking B on her report card. Delaney Martin was everything she was perceived to be. She was studious, quiet, and weak.

Oh, there were times when she flashed some fire, but I saw now that those times were more small sparks than real fire. If she had real fire in her, she wouldn't have smiled for that fucking picture.

When she first called, I hadn't answered, and I hadn't answered the second, third, fourth, or fifth time she called. I deleted her texts and voicemails as soon as my phone beeped with their notifications. I didn't want to hear anything the weak bitch had to say. And, even if I had wanted to hear her excuses and explanations, I didn't want to do it over the phone.

And, now, I was five beers and three shots in at the party wondering just how far I was going to have to take this to forget Delaney's betrayal. I figured I'd have to dip into the party favors before the end of the night in order to forget this fucked-up day, but I was okay with that. I've snorted up coke before for a lot less.

We were all sitting on the boulder we usually hang out on when we're partying at the cove. Sands Cove had an inlet where the beach was smattered with a bunch of different-sized boulders, and we usually made use of the boulders as tables and chairs.

At often times, beds too.

And it was while we were congregated around our boulder that Melissa sauntered up to me reminding me of the last time I attended a party here. "Hey, Deke," she greeted, smiling. She gave everyone else a quick glance. "Hey, guys."

She was greeted with polite hellos, but you could tell the girls were super tense about her approach because they knew. They knew where this was going, and I couldn't even summon enough love for them, at the moment, to care how hurt their feelings were going to be by the end of the night.

Melissa returned her attention to me. "So, uhm, where's Delaney?" she asked.

I smirked, the alcohol helping to dull what I was really feeling. "In New Hampshire with her boyfriend," I huffed. "They're being in love and planning their future together." Melissa looked confused, and I realized she wasn't the type to appreciate sarcasm.

"But...I thought you were her boyfriend?" she asked.

The girls were going to hate me but fuck it. "Nope," I replied, popping the 'p'. "She was a challenge. I de-virginized and dirtied her, and now I'm done." I could hear Emerson's and Linnie's gasps, but I wouldn't look at them. Maybe it was chicken shit because I knew they'd forgive me eventually, but I didn't look their way. I didn't owe Delaney Martin a motherfucking thing.

Melissa took that as an invitation to sit on my lap. "So, then...you're free to...hang out?"

Ignoring Melissa, Roselyn said, "Don't do this, Deke."

I finally looked over at my friends and I focused on Linnie. "Don't, what?" I smirked. "Don't enjoy uncomplicated pussy?"

She straightened her back and I could tell she wanted to rip into me, but we didn't do that. We didn't air our grievances for the masses. Our group was tight and private. Linnie would wait to yell at me later. I glanced over at Emerson, and her face was stoic; expressionless.

I looked back at Melissa nestled on my lap and, admittedly, it felt wrong. *She* felt wrong in my arms, but I didn't give a fuck. I needed to forget Delaney's betrayal, and booze, drugs, and women were the only way to do that.

Suddenly, there was a shift in the air.

I could feel the change all around me. I glanced over at the group and they were all standing up, backs erect, faces serious, and chins up. There's only one reason they'd be on guard like that.

Winston and Delaney must be here.

When I turned my head in the opposite direction, it wasn't Winston and Delaney coming down the hill towards us; it was Delaney and Ava.

I watched as their heads swiveled every which way, presumably looking for me, but I stayed seated with Melissa on my lab.

Like hell I would run to her.

When Delaney's eyes finally landed on mine, her entire body stilled. I watched as she took in Melissa on my lap and I couldn't have timed it more perfectly if I had tried. Ava was standing behind her, and when my eyes glanced her way, she looked furious.

That's rich.

Delaney snapped out of her shock, and made her way down, but her steps were small and unsure. When she stopped in front of us, it was a full thirty seconds before she tore her eyes away from a smug-looking Melissa and looked at me. "I...I take it you didn't read my texts?" she asked, her voice steadier than I thought it'd be. "You didn't...listen to the voicemails?"

My chin jutted out and my hands found their way to Melissa's thighs. "No," I replied, making sure my face and voice were void of any emotion, whatsoever.

"Are you drunk?" she asked, her eyes narrowing a bit.

"Not even close," I answered, which was true. Delaney's appearance sobered up whatever little buzz I had going.

"Deke, I can expl-"

I laughed, and it wasn't a friendly laugh either. "Delaney, there's nothing to explain," I assured her. "A picture's worth a thousand words, right?"

Her brown eyes stared deeply into my green ones for a few tense seconds before she pulled a new-looking phone from her back pocket, fiddled with the screen, aimed it at me and Melissa, and snapped a picture. I watched as her fingers dance across the screen, presumably saving the photo.

"What the fuck did you take that for?" I asked, my voice faltering a bit and letting the rage peek through.

Delaney lifted her chin before saying, "Because you're right. Because when you...when you find out you were wrong and call me to beg for forgiveness, that's the first thing I'll see. I'll see that picture behind the phone ringing, and it'll remind me not to answer your call."

Now that the rage had seeped through in my voice, it was hard to rein it all back in. My hands slid from the outside of Melissa's thighs to in the inside, and since she was wearing shorts, my hands were splayed across her soft skin. "You're out of your mind if you think I'm going to call you for anything when I have *this* available to me."

I wasn't sure what I was expecting, but Delaney giving me a tight nod and walking away from me wasn't it.

However, she wasn't going to get off that easily.

CHAPTER 32

Delaney ~

The pain was just like they sing about in sad love songs.

It was…*consuming.*

Deke hadn't even given me a chance to explain before moving on to another girl. Well, I guess going back to another girl would be more accurate. After all, he's had Melissa before.

I knew he was going to be pissed, but I really believed he'd hear me out first before appointing himself judge, jury, and executioner.

I believed he loved me.

And, Christ, I didn't need that stupid picture of him and Melissa on my phone. I knew I'd never get the image of her on his lap with his hands wrapped around her thighs out of my head *ever.*

When my plane had been getting ready to land, I had texted Ava, and true to her word, she had met me at the airport. As soon as I told her Deke wasn't answering any of my texts or messages, she told me there was a party at the cove, and suggested we try there first. The only messaged I had received was from my Dad asking me what the hell I was thinking.

I ignored it.

Ava had driven like a bat out of hell to get back to Sands Cove, and when we got to the cove, I had never imagined I find Deke with another girl.

I pictured drunk. I pictured furious. I even pictured drugs.

I never pictured another girl.

And out of all the girls he could have been with, why did it have to be Melissa? I already had a mental picture of them together from that first night, I didn't need a reminder of…how good they were together.

The second my eyes locked onto his hands squeezing her thighs, I knew I wasn't strong enough to do this. I turned and fled like a coward.

Too bad I didn't get far.

Ava had been right next to me storming off back towards her car, but I was pulled up short from my left side by a hard, masculine hand. Deke whirled me around to face him, and in that move, I noticed the entire party had stopped what they were doing to witness the showdown between Deke Marlow and mousy, little Delaney Martin.

Deke bore down on me and gone was the impassive mask he had on. He looked murderous and a part of me felt vindicated at his loss of control. Of course, that came to a quick halt with the words he spewed next. "You think just because your pussy was unused that it's special or something?" he taunted viciously. "You think that just because you let me use you up like a desperate whore, I'll come running back to you when Reynolds is busy with a better, *experienced* cunt?"

"Deke!" Roselyn cried, but I didn't know why she bothered. It's not like she didn't already know that Ramsey, Liam, and Deke were fallen angels.

He ignored her outburst, and that's when I knew it was over. Deke adored Roselyn and Emerson, and for him to ignore either of them said so much. Deke's face was pure evil when he added, "I'm sure Reynolds will be happy to know I was too busy teaching you how to suck dick and be a decent fuck to take your ass. Maybe you can give him that on your honeymoon since the rest of you reeks of my cum."

Rage was nothing in the face of pain.

Nothing.

Pain was crippling while rage was fleeting.

Hearing Deke tell everyone the private stuff we did and the fact that I was no good at it was...debilitating. I was immobile with shock at his cruelty, as was everyone else, I think.

Everyone but Ava.

"You motherfucker!" she screamed. "I'm going to fucking kill you."

There were some scuffling sounds behind me, but I was too...stuck to look back to see what was going on. My mind was processing that Ava probably charged and someone was holding her back, but the noises and screams were faded garble; like my head was underwater or something.

And just when I thought Deke couldn't hurt me any worse..."Oh, and I almost forgot," he sneered. "If the worst happens because you were too stupid and inexperienced to protect yourself, tell the clinic to just charge it to my tab."

Have you ever felt your heart tear in half?

It happens, you know.

It really, truly happens.

The words he can never take back sent me into such a vortex of uncontrollable emotions, and I did the one thing I never saw myself doing.

I attacked Deke Marlow.

Fists formed, and I launched myself at Deke striking him anywhere I could make contact. "You sonofabitch!" I screamed. "You no good fucking sonofabitch!" I could hear people yelling my name, and I felt...enclosed, but I was too busy attacking Deke to take in what was going on around us. "I fucking *hate* you!"

I couldn't see past my tears, but it didn't take Deke any effort at all to subdue me, and I heard him say, "Not half as much as I hate you."

I pulled back and looked up into his face not caring that he could see into my nothingness; the hollowness I felt. I looked up at him and I felt it; real, unadulterated *hate*.

With all my might, I jerked out of his hold and took a step back. My face was a mess, and my voice was scratchy, but I didn't care when I said, "Don't ever come near me again, Deke. *Ever.*"

He had already humiliated me beyond comprehension, so I didn't care if everyone saw me running away from him. I ran until I was at Ava's car and it wasn't seconds later when she was unlocking the doors and we were getting in, burning the tires in our haste to leave.

Everything was a blur from leaving the party to arriving at Ava's. I couldn't even recall getting out of the car and making my way to her bedroom. But, once I sat down on her bed, every emotion I've experienced in all my life came pouring out until I collapsed in tormented cries on her bed.

Ava's arms held me as I exhausted every tear I was capable of producing, and it wasn't until the next morning, that I told her I was going to lose everything, and I had nowhere to go.

She had driven me to the bank where we spent all morning withdrawing every damn dime from my account. I hadn't bothered with my appearance, and since I looked like a punching bag with swollen eyes, I think the bank manager felt sorry for me, and didn't ask any questions or give me a hard time.

After withdrawing all my money, we had driven to Manotile, one town over, and opened a new bank account in my name only with a bank my parents didn't partner with. Once my account was all set up, Ava had driven me to a car dealership to buy a car, and for the first time in my life, price mattered. While I had a shit ton of money, I knew it wouldn't last forever, so I had to...plan.

There was also the fact that, after a lot of arguing with Ava about staying with her, I needed to find a place to live. My parents hadn't officially kicked me out yet, but I was still ignoring their calls and messages, along with Winston's and his parents. It was only a matter of time before the threats started, so I needed to be one step ahead of them.

In my new, but economical little Toyota, Ava went her way back to Sands Cove as I stayed in Manotile looking for a small house or something. Originally, I had planned on staying in Sands Cove, but that was before Deke had demolished my soul. There was no way I could show my face at Windsor anymore, but that was okay. All those years of having no life and living in the library were going to finally pay off. I could miss the rest of the school year and still graduate. Not with straight-A's, but with a solid B average. I just had to call the school on Monday, and since I was already an adult, they didn't need my parents' approval, and I could graduate and get my certificate without the ceremony.

After hours of looking, I finally found a small cottage style house on the outskirts of Manotile, and I contacted the realtor. The second I offered cash, the house was as good as mine.

I drove back to Ava's, where we spent the night looking at furniture online. When I pointed out that I needed to be frugal until I got a job, Ava had announced all the furniture would be on her and she didn't want to hear another word about it.

We avoided all talk Deke, and by the time I was wrapped up in her bed, her arms around me again, I had half convinced myself I was going to be okay.

However, lying there in the dark, I couldn't stop my mind from doing a mental countdown. I had only one week before my period was due.

One week.

One week, and life would cut me some slack or it would ruin me further.

I already knew I'd never get an abortion if I did turn up pregnant, and so that fuckening was akin to Armageddon, because my life would be altered forever.

And there's no way Deke Marlow would ever know about it.

CHAPTER 33

Deke ~

It was Thursday after third period and Delaney still hadn't made an appearance at school. I'd seen Winston, but I kept my distance. I didn't want Delaney, or anyone, thinking I still gave a fuck.

But I did.

I cared because, after Delaney had run from me, Emerson and Roselyn had looked at me with so much disgust, things were still tense between us, five days later.

I also cared because, regardless of the show I put on Friday, my love for Delaney hadn't been fleeting. I truly loved her and still did.

Luckily for me, betrayal trumped love.

The only other issue I had was that I had become worrisome at Delaney's absence. Being the kind of student she was, I couldn't see her risking graduation, and that's how I found myself at Ava's locker knowing she wanted my balls on a skewer.

"Ava," I called out, approaching her.

She shut her locker and turned to face me. "Deke," she acknowledged, and her...emotionless voice had the hairs on the back of my neck standing up.

"So, she's willing to risk graduating?" I hedged.

The tip of Ava's lip lifted, and she looked like the Mob boss I always likened her to. "Delaney's already graduated, Deke," she said, dropping that little bomb.

"What?"

Ava's face was pure satisfaction when she said, "What do you want, Deke? My good graces are the only thing keeping you on your feet, so say what you want to and then leave me the fuck alone."

Her good graces?

Yeah, right.

I stepped to her. "And what exactly is it you think you can do to me, Ava?" I dared.

Her eyes never faltered as she reached into the breast pocket of her uniform and produced her phone. "I'll tell you exactly what I'm going to do to you, Deke," she mocked before she looked down at her phone, her fingers flying everywhere, and then bringing it up to my face.

My eyes darted to the picture on her phone, and it was that fucking picture of Delaney with Winston and their parents. I looked back at Ava. "What?" I snapped. "I've already seen that fucking picture."

Her smile was positively lethal when she said, "Look closer, Deke."

I didn't want to, but I looked back at the picture on her phone, and that's when I saw it. The caption was missing. "There's no caption," I said.

"Look closer to the post, Deke," she said, her voice villainous. "Like...maybe check the *date* of this post." I snatched her phone from her hand, and studying the photo, I saw what she was referring to.

The date of the picture and post was last year in March.

Last fucking year.

Reynolds fucking played me.

Ava could tell the second it registered because she plucked her phone from my hand and smiled before saying, *"That's* what I'm going to do to you, Deke Marlow." She put her phone back in her pocket and wrapped her arms around her book, hugging it to her chest, looking positively giddy. "Delaney didn't want me to say anything, but since she's move on, why not?" She said, shrugging her shoulder. "Delaney's parents ambushed her with the Reynolds in New Hampshire and when she realized it, she decided to finish the tour, but was going to come home. She tried to call you, but she lost her phone. After the tour, she went and bought a new phone, only to answer a call from me telling her what was going one. She jumped on the first flight out of New Hampshire to get to you so she could explain." Ava cocked her head. "And what did you do? You fucked Melissa Randall after telling Delaney to get an abortion if there ends up being a little bit of residue from your relationship."

"I never fucked Mel-"

Ava's laugh cut me off. "Does it even matter?" she challenged. "You threw away the best thing that will ever happen to you, Deke. I don't need to do shit to you because that regret...that...*erosion* is going to stay with you forever." Her true words were making it hard to breathe. "Delaney's going to move on with someone who is going to love *and* trust her, and she's going to be happy, Deke. She's going to be happy despite you and that's enough for me." She took a step back, and she looked joyous. "Oh, and another thing, if Delaney sucks in bed, it's because she had a horrible teacher. Her next lover should be able to fix that."

Ava walked off before I had a chance to kill her.

Because I really, really wanted to.

I wanted to snuff the life out of her until her words lost their truth.

I stood there feeling as if my chest was caving in; like my heart was being crushed.

If what Ava said was true-and she had no reason to lie-Delaney hadn't chosen her family over me. Delaney had chosen me, and I...

My back dropped against the row of lockers with the significance of what I did to her. All week long I had held on to my righteous anger, not letting anything else in, but now...now that I no longer had a right to be angry, everything I said and did to her that night burned in my mind like an iron left unattended.

And, Christ Almighty, I actually told her to put her abortion on my fucking *tab*.

I made her believe getting pregnant by me was nothing special. I announced to damn near the entire school that Delaney let me fuck her without protection. I blasted all of her private moments to everyone.

Ava was right.

I hadn't trusted Delaney.

I fired off a group text to Ramsey, Liam, Linnie, and Emerson that I was leaving school and I'd fill them in later right as I stormed out of the building.

I needed to find Delaney.

I let out a pathetic laugh because she had been right all along, too. She knew the truth would come out sooner or later and she knew I'd be begging for forgiveness. My stomach soured with how I wanted to call her but couldn't. Knowing that picture she took of Melissa on my lap would be what popped up if I called her is the only thing that kept me from calling her.

I drove to her house thinking about how that picture of her and Winston had made me feel and knew that I could never take away what seeing Melissa on my lap did to her. I did the one thing you just can't do to a girl. I shoved another girl in her face.

Delaney was already insecure with my status in this town, reducing her and what we had to nothing was the worst thing I could do to her-to *us*.

I had to pull over onto the side of the road.

Everything I did to her Saturday night kept playing over, and over again in my head and I couldn't escape the sickness. I wondered how Ramsey lived with it; with what he did to Emerson way back when. I might have crossed some serious lines with Delaney, but I had never put her health in jeopardy, and I seriously wondered how Ramsey lived with himself. If what I was feeling was an indication of what I'd feel for the rest of my life, I'd rather put a bullet through my brain.

Ava's taunting comment about how Delaney's next lover would be better churned in my gut. I could live with losing her to Reynolds because she was his before I came into the picture, but to see her with someone else?

I leaped out of the car and almost threw up on the side of the road when I pictured Delaney pregnant with another man's baby after aborting mine because I told her to.

Jesus Christ.

I couldn't do this. I grabbed my phone from my pocket and dialed Ramsey. He answered on the second ring. "Deke?" Then I heard him faintly telling the teacher he had to take the call.

I gave him a few seconds to clear the classroom before I said, "I fucked up, man."

I could feel Ramsey's stillness over the phone. "Where do you need us?" he asked, ready and willing to save me.

"It's not like that," I muttered, my mouth dry. I had to take a couple of deep breaths before I was able to tell him everything. I told him about approaching Ava because I was worried. I told him about Ava showing me the old post. I told him how Delaney had come home to me. I told him everything. When I was finished, I confessed, "I think I'm losing my mind, Ram."

His was voice serious and absolute as he said, "It'll never go away, Deke." I knew what he meant. He was talking about how I treated Delaney Saturday night. "If you do this…if you chase after her," he stressed, "you'll be living on your knees for the rest of your life where she's concerned."

I thought about his words. "And how does that make you feel?"

Ramsey let out a soft laugh. "Emerson is so vital to my existence, I'd *crawl* after her if I had to in order to keep her in my life, Deke. After what I did to her…I'll take whatever she grants me."

"I know what you mean," I said solemnly.

Because I did.

CHAPTER 34

Delaney ~

It's been five days, and the wound was still fresh. And I'm not talking about scabbed up with the edges itching either. I'm talking about still bleeding fresh.

Luckily, I've spent the past few days receiving furniture deliveries and have exhausted all my time-and Ava's time-furnishing my new home. It's been kind of fun actually, and we've managed to avoid any and all social media.

I got an email finalizing my high school diploma, and it'll be mailed to me in a couple of weeks. I also got my period yesterday, and the relief had swept my legs right out from under me. It was the only time I've cried uncontrollably since that first night.

I've ignored all calls from my parents and Winston and the only reason I was back at my parents' home was because I needed to finally pack up the rest of my belongings. Admittedly, there wasn't much, but I had lots of memorabilia I wanted to take with me.

There were countless photos of me and Ava throughout the years, academic awards, and even some sports trophies from my younger years.

I had driven over this morning, and it was taking me longer than I thought to pack, but with the housekeeping staff used to being invisible, no one questioned what I was doing home.

My parents still weren't any wiser to the fact that I had emptied my bank account because I had received a notification of a recent deposit. The deposits were set up to deposit into the account bi-weekly, and so if my parents had any inkling as to what I've been up to, they would have put a stop to the deposits. I had no shame, though. The second the notification had come through, I had driven to Sands Cove and withdrew the recent deposit. This time I had been dealing with a different customer service representative, and since I didn't look like death warmed over like last time, she was a little more leery about my withdrawal. It won't be too long before someone at the bank notifies my parents of the account activity.

Everything came to a pause when Winston's car swerved into my driveway during one of my many trips to my new car.

I left the trunk open, not bothering to hide what I was doing, and watched Winston get out of his car and slam the door shut.

When he was standing in front of me, he barked, "Where in the fuck have you been?"

I stared up at the boy I once considered a friend and all I saw was greedy betrayal. He had conspired with my parents to break me and Deke up, but he had done more than that. He had helped destroy everything I believed love to be. Sure, he couldn't have guessed things would turn out as viciously as they had, but that didn't matter. He chose to join my parents in being deceitful and I couldn't look at him the same anymore.

I crossed my arms over my chest. "That's none of your business," I replied coolly.

He ignored my response. "You just leave New Hampshire and tell no one," he chastised. "Your parents were worr-"

I dropped my arms. "Oh, stop it, Winston," I snapped. "You and I both know my parents couldn't care less where I'm at or what I'm doing. They were just pissed their little ambush didn't work."

"Jesus Christ, Delaney," he swore. "Why can't you just stop it? Why can't you just stop being so selfish for a second and think about what you're doing to all of our lives?"

"Me, selfish?" I screeched. "Are you serious? I'm being selfish because I want to be happy in life? Are you kidding me, Winston?!"

And then he confessed something I had no idea about. "Your parents are broke, Delaney," he yelled, revealing the ugly truth. "Your dad has a gambling problem, and he's on the verge of losing everything."

"You're lying," I whispered, stung and hurt.

Winston ran his hands through his hair, and lifting his face to the sky, roared to the Heavens, and I knew he was telling me the truth. He looked back down at me and said, "It's true, Delaney. He has a gambling problem, and your mother either doesn't know or doesn't care."

I tried to process the words, but in the middle of realizing he was telling me the absolute truth, something else occurred to me. "What do your parents get out of this, Winston?" I asked. "What do they get out of this besides the partnership they always hinted to?"

"Delaney-"

"Tell me!"

He was quiet for so long, I didn't think he was going to answer me, but he finally said, "There'd be no pre-nup, Delaney. Your father changed his will to leave every patent and discovery to you. Our marriage gives my dad the right to everything medical breakthrough your father has ever been involved in."

I shook my head. "No," I whispered in denial. "If it's all mine, then it would go to our children, or you if-"

This time, it was Winston shaking his head at me. "As your husband with no pre-nup, I'd have the right to sign everything over to my dad."

The breath left my body and the edges of my sight faded in and out. My parents were broke, and Winston's parents were going to bail them out using me as the currency. This wasn't an arranged marriage to strengthen two dynasties.

This was extortion.

Oh, it might have started out that way when we were ten and the agreement was made, but Winston's father was clearly more craftier than my own.

Ava.

Ava had a horrible reputation for being a bitch and a whore. She did drugs without a care in the world, and she played with guys no matter who was watching. She was beautiful, wild, ferocious, and wonton with no regard to what people thought of her.

She was, by all accounts, these horrible things, but she's the only person in all my life who has loved me, defended me, and stood by me unconditionally, asking for nothing in return.

Meanwhile, the people with reputed reputations of class, money, pedigree, strength, and power were the weak ones who have used me and let me down time, and time again.

Fuck. These. Assholes.

"Well, it doesn't matter what our parents had planned, Winston," I replied. "It's over. All of it, it's over. I want nothing to do with you, your parents, or even my parents."

"You can't mean that, Delaney," he clipped out. "How will you live?" Spoken like a true spoiled, entitled piece of garbage.

I found my first genuine smile in days as I said, "I'm going to work. I'm going to work, earn an honest living, and surround myself with people who want what's best for me-not them."

"Delaney, if I don't get you to-"

I barked out a humorless laugh. Of course, he was only here because he was at risk of losing something. *"It's over, Winston,"* I said, each word stressed with meaning. "As soon as I pack my last bag, I'm out of Sands Cove."

His eyes popped, and he reared his head back. "You can't be serious?"

All of the sudden, I realized I didn't owe Winston any more of my time. I didn't owe anyone in this town anything. Ava and the housekeeping staff were about the only people in the world who warranted my respect.

But there was one thing I wanted to know. "Who posted that picture, Winston?" I asked. "Was it you or my mother?" I wasn't sure he was going to fess up, so I said, "You owe me." By now, he had to have heard about what had gone down at the cove.

He sighed before admitting, "I...I doctored the picture for your mom, but she's the one who posted and tagged it everywhere."

I figured that's what had happened. I wasn't surprised, but I was disappointed that his words still brought out an emotional response from me.

"I need to get back to what I was doing, Winston," I said, my voice defeated but...substantial; strong.

"Delaney-"

Whatever he was about to say was cut off by a white Lexus racing up the driveway behind my car, and all I could think of at a time like this, was how at least Winston was courteous enough to not block my car in when he drove up.

How silly.

Winston and I stood side by side was we both watched Deke Marlow get out of his car and stomp up the driveway.

It hurt.

It fucking hurt to just *look* at him.

I was going to need more than five days to steel myself against the love I, regrettably, still felt for him.

CHAPTER 35

Deke ~

Seeing Delaney standing next to Reynolds took me back to the day she aligned herself with him at school and I had kicked his ass. Only, this time, I was in the wrong here, and Reynolds was irrelevant.

Ignoring Winston, my eyes ran over Delaney from head to toe and back up again, and she looked exhausted; lifeless.

I wasn't any good at this sort of thing, so I did what I always did when I wanted something...

I took it.

"We need to talk," I told her.

Before she could reply, Reynolds tried to play at being her hero again, and that was all it took to make me snap. "Deke, Delan-"

I threw my left then followed up with my right hook. He fell back and as soon as his ass landed on the grass, I was on top of him. But before I could get a third hit in, Delaney had thrown herself in between us, shielding him, forcing my arm to reach back and drop.

"Are you insane?!" she screamed. "What is the matter with you?!"

"He doesn't belong here!" I roared.

"Neither do you!" she yelled back.

I stood up, grabbed her arm, and yanked her to me. "You either go in the house with me right now, so we can talk, or I will, swear to fucking God, kill him, Delaney." I wasn't exaggerating either. Searching for her as my life fell apart all around me, only to find her with Reynolds, was fucking me up.

Her beautiful chocolate eyes rounded in outrage. "How dare you?! You have no right-"

I dropped her arm and whirled back around towards Winston to finish the job. Before I could reach him, Delaney threw herself in front of me to block me. "Stop it!"

"You're always trying to fucking save him, Delaney," I yelled. "Why?!"

"I'm not trying to save him," she argued. "I'm trying to end this bullshit!"

"Then go inside and talk to me!" I demanded. Out of the corner of my eye I could see Winston slowly getting up and I wanted so badly to knock the motherfucker back down.

Delaney faced Winston and said, "Winston, you need to leave."

"But-"

"Leave, Winston," she repeated. "And understand I don't ever want to see you again. *Ever.*"

My heart was thundering inside my chest because I was sure I was next. She didn't have any reason to hate Winston more than she hated me and her voice was ice cold and unfeeling as she spoke to him. His eyes shot to mine and he must have believed what he saw in them, because he gave Delaney a tight nod and walked towards his car to leave.

The second his car was out of sight, I turned back to Delaney. "Baby, I-"

The slap was so powerful, my head snapped sideways causing a wave of heat to shoot up my neck.

But I deserved it.

I deserved that, and so much more.

"Don't ever call me that again," Delaney seethed. "I thought I told you I never wanted to see you again, Deke. What are you doing here?"

My face stung like a motherfucker, but I'd let her hit me again if that's what she needed to do to purge out all her hate and hurt. "I know, Delaney," I replied. "Ava told me everything."

She didn't look surprised at all over that little announcement. Delaney had adopted a hell of a poker face, and I hated it. "So?"

There were a million things I could say to her to try to excuse my behavior, but the truth was, there *was* no excuse. I hadn't trusted her, and that's where I failed her. I hadn't trusted her and, in doing so, I lumped her in with the group of people who weren't trustworthy, and that was wrong of me.

So very fucking wrong of me.

I had nothing but naked honestly to offer her. "Tell me what I have to do, Lamb," I replied.

Gone was her poker face. Now, she looked murderous. "Do *not* call me that," she snarled. "I am not your lamb. I am not your *anything.*"

"Tell me what I have to do, Lamb," I repeated because she was my lamb. She was my lamb and I'll crawl behind her for the rest of my life just like Ramsey said if she forgives me. I'm pretty sure I'll crawl behind her even if she doesn't forgive me.

"What you have to do for what, Deke?" she asked, stepping away from me and giving herself some space.

"To get you to forgive me," I replied simply.

Delaney's eyes widened a fraction of a second before she let out a hurtful, bitter laugh. "Are you serious?" she asked incredulously. "Do you honestly think, for one second, I would ever *forgive* you for what you did to me?" Her brows drew downward. "Do you truly believe I'd forgive you for humiliating me the way you did? For flaunting Melissa in my face? For not trusting me? For telling everyone I'm horrible in bed? For telling me to abort your *mistake?*"

I flinched at that.

Every word was like the lash of a whip. A lash I deserved for what I did to her.

But I couldn't let guilt distract me from my goal here. I knew I didn't deserve her forgiveness. I knew she deserved better. I knew I'd never be worthy.

But that didn't matter.

I was struggling with living without her when I thought she had betrayed me, so knowing she hadn't?

There was no way I was letting her go.

"Tell me what to do," I repeated.

"Leave me alone," she responded, certain of her answer. "Leave me alone and never bother me again, Deke."

"I can't do that," I told her honestly.

"Well, then I don't know what to tell you, because that's all I want from you," she said again.

"Delaney, I'm sorry. I-"

"I don't want you to be sorry!" she yelled, dropping her cold act. "I don't want an apology from you! I want you to leave me alone, Deke. I want you gone from my life, my memories, my *everything!*"

I refused to believe that. I had to. I'd lose my mind otherwise. "And if you're pregnant?"

I watched her spine snap straight, and pure loathing crawled across her beautiful features. "Then I'll charge it to your tab," she said, throwing my words back in my face.

"You'd really do that?" Intellectually, I knew there was nothing I could do about what choices she made regarding her body. Emotionally, I knew I deserved her words and that threat. But I couldn't bring myself to believe she'd really do that.

Her eyes started to shine, and I knew she hated the idea as much as I did. "Luckily, we never have to find out," she said, gracing me with a mercy I hadn't granted her. "I started my period yesterday."

I stepped towards her, but she matched my step and move back from me. "Delaney, I'll do whatever you ask of me, except leave you alone," I told her. "I fucked up. I know that, and you'll never know how sorry I am. But I love yo-"

"Don't," she spat. "Do not tell me you love me. You don't love me, Deke. You don't know the first thing about love and how to love someone."

"That's not true," I argued.

Delaney took a deep breath and I could see my presence taking a toll on her. "I'll never forgive you, Deke. I'll never forgive you, and I don't want anything to do with you. I want to forget you ever tainted my life, and I want to go on to be with someone who…well, who's not you."

I had my hands wrapped around her upper arms and shook her in desperation. "No one else will ever have you, Delaney," I snarled, and it didn't matter that I was in the wrong. "You're mine. You're mine, and I'm sorry I didn't take good care of you. I'm sorry I…couldn't see past my jealousy and insecurities to treat you the way you deserve to be treated. But I am not letting you go, Lamb. *Ever.*" Tears started streaming down her face and they gave me hope. She had to feel something besides hate for me if she was crying, right?

Wrong.

"I don't love you anymore, Deke," she said, slicing me in half. "I don't think I ever loved you or else I don't think I would have been able to move on from you so quickly."

She was lying.

She had to be lying.

I fucked up, and she was just punishing me by telling me these…*lies.*

"You don't love me?"

Delaney shook her head. "No, Deke, I don't."

CHAPTER 36

Delaney ~

I was lying.

I was very much in love with Deke still, but it wasn't enough.

There was no way I'd be able to forget and forgive what he did to me.

I wasn't as strong as Emerson.

I also knew I needed to get away from him, because every second he stood there was a threat to my pride and my sanity.

Deke damaged me with what he did, and I didn't feel as if I'd ever be able to trust him again. "Deke, I...I have to go. I need to finish packing and-"

His head reared back, shocked. *"Packing?"*

Shit.

I hadn't meant to let him in on my plans, but what did it matter. Regardless of what he was professing, he couldn't stop me from leaving, and I could always get a restraining order on him if I had to.

"It's not your business, Deke," I replied, needing to get away from him.

His hold on my arms tightened. "Everything about you is my business, Delaney," he fumed. "Christ, Delaney. I'm so fucking *sorry*. Tell me what to do, and I will fucking do it!"

I wasn't ready to sheath my claws yet. I cocked my head and asked, "Let me ask you something, Deke. What happens if I forgive you?"

His hands dropped from my arms and he slid them into the front pockets of his school uniform. He and Winston had obviously ditched school to harass me. "What do you mean?" he asked, slightly confused. "If you forgive me...well, we put this behind us and be together like we're supposed to be."

God, men really were clueless.

"So, what happens the first time you reach over to touch me, and all I see is your hand on Melissa's thigh instead of mine?" Deke paled, but I didn't relent. "What happens the first time you join me in bed, and I lock up because I don't know what I'm doing? What happens when you get brave enough to finally try anal sex, and all I can think about is Winston while you're inside me?"

"Stop it, Delaney," he snapped.

"What happens the first time there's a pregnancy scare, and I can't tell you because your solution to the problem is to run down to the clinic?"

"I said, *stop it*," he begged.

"Or how about the first time another guy tells me I'm beautiful, and I believe him because I will *always* feel inadequate around you?" The last thing in the world I'd ever want to be is a cheater, but even though the digs were designed to hurt Deke, that didn't make them any less true. Deke's attacked against me had been personal, and his aim had been true.

Before I knew what he was about, Deke's hands shot out, grabbed my face and he crushed his lips to mine. He kissed me like he did that day next to his car when he gave me the safety pin. He was kissing me with so much emotion, I felt powerless to resist.

I felt powerless to resist because I was pathetic, and I wanted this kiss to undo everything. I wanted the pain to go away so badly that I opened up and let him in.

The next few minutes were nothing but crashing and burning with desperation and fear. Desperate to forget the past few days, and fear because we knew we wouldn't be able to. It wasn't until I heard a door shut behind me that the fog of lust lifted, and I noticed that Deke had walked us back into the house.

I broke off the kiss trying to get a grip on where this was going. "Deke-"

"No, Delaney," he snapped. "You're mine. You're fucking mine and you can't tell me to stop."

As confused, hurt, angry, and lonely as I was, I still wasn't without complete sense. "Deke, we can't," I breathed as he started sucking on my neck; marking me. "I'm on my period," I reminded him.

His answer was to drag me to the nearest guest bathroom and plop me on the counter. Stepping in between my spread thighs, he growled, "Do you think I give a fuck if you're bleeding or not?"

Evidently not.

But that wasn't my biggest issue. I'd been letting Deke do whatever he wanted to do to me since the first night I slept with him. I always knew my period wasn't anything that was ever going to deter him. "Deke, stop it!" I said more forcefully.

I knew Deke Marlow was dark. I knew he was ruthless. I knew he was relentless. And I knew he was…evil.

I knew it.

But I never knew just how dark he was or how evil his soul was until he grabbed me by my chin and said, "I'm taking you, Delaney, whether you want me to or not." I gasped as his hold tightened on my face. I could literally *feel* the darkness swimming in his veins shimmer over me. "I own you. I own you like I have receipt for you in my back pocket."

"Deke–"

"You're mine," he repeated. "You're mine and I will make this right, I swear to God. I will undo everything I did to you, but you will *not* tell me no. And there's no way I'm every going to let you leave me."

My hands pushed at his chest. "Fuck you! You can't undo it!"

His hand wrapped around my neck and he squeezed. "Then you shouldn't have kissed me back!" he roared in my face, right before he started tearing at my shorts.

The fight was on.

I knew I wasn't going to win, but I had to fight. I couldn't just give in no matter how much my heart wanted to. My heart wanted to forgive him, but my mind wanted to make him pay.

And my soul?

My soul wanted to feel the peace only being with Deke could bring me.

Deke had yanked me off the counter and, even after fighting with all my might, he had my shorts and panties down around my knees right before he swung me around, pressing me up against the countertop. He locked his right arm around my body as his left hand reached in between my legs and he pulled my tampon out.

It was the most intimately disgusting thing anyone has ever done to me.

"Deke!" I screamed, trying to make him see reason, but he was beyond reason. Not two seconds later, he drove into me, and the moisture from my blood allowed him to slip right in. *"Oh, God!"*

Deke slammed into me as if he hadn't just forced himself into my body. "You're mine, Delaney," he grunted. "You're mine, and I will not live without you." I started crying the second I knew he was starting to win. "I love you, Delaney. I love you more than my own life, and I will…I will…anything, Lamb. Tell me, and I'll do anything."

I couldn't tell him.

I couldn't do anything other than ride the wave and I felt weak at how I could enjoy what he was doing to me. I hated how I knew I was going to forgive him. I hated that I was going to be that girl. I hated how he felt so good inside me, all common sense ceased to exist.

"Deke…" I cried, not bother to hide the tears.

His hand grabbed my neck, and he pulled my body up against his as he rammed his cock into me over, and over again. "I love you," he panted. I stared at him through the mirror, and he looked as torn up as I felt. "I love you, Delaney. I'm sorry, baby. I'm so fucking sorry."

And then I felt it.

The signs of what was to come and shame coursed through my body as my body started to respond to his thrusts. I felt the anguish down to my soul as I told him, "I'm going to cum…"

His hold on my neck tightened and his head dropped to my shoulder as his thrusts became harder, faster, and deeper. "Cum on my cock, baby," he begged. "Cum on my cock and show me I haven't lost you completely."

I came and my scream could be heard all over the house. *"Deke!"*

A few grunts later, Deke was emptying himself inside me, until I felt the weight of his body collapse over me. Our chests heaved with exertion, and while I was absolutely wrecked, being a girl, I couldn't ignore the fact I was bleeding.

"Deke?" He mumbled something against my back, but I couldn't make it out. "Deke, I need to shower."

He righted himself and looking at me in the mirror said, "I can't let you go, Delaney."

"Deke, I just need to show-"

"No," he hissed. "You can't...I can't let you out of my sight until you say it."

"Say what?" Deke let out a deep breath before slipping out of me and the moistness was beyond what I was comfortable with. I was going to bleed all over this floor if I didn't do something. "Let me shower, and then we can talk, okay?"

He looked skeptical but nodded. "Okay."

Deke redressed me, and the blood not bothering him shined a huge light on his psychopathy.

CHAPTER 37

Deke ~

It was done, but I knew it still wouldn't be enough to undo everything I did to Delaney Saturday night, but I knew I had to do something. I also deleted that fucking picture of Melissa and me off her phone and cloud backup.

We had showered together because we both needed to get clean, but I wouldn't have cared either way. It wasn't until I re-dressed, and she went in search for clothing, that I noticed the two boxes on the floor of her bedroom, and that most of her personal effects were missing.

I had felt paralyzed with the realization that Delaney had been packing to move when I showed up earlier. She was moving, and had I not shown up when I did, she would have been lost to me. There's no way Ava would ever tell me where she lived.

After Delaney had dressed, she sat next to me on her bed to talk, but as I stroked her back, she fell asleep. Now she was laying across her bed, her head in my lap, as I had done my best not to wake her while I made the video.

I was sitting up on her bed with my back against the headboard, but I had done my best to make sure it was visible that we were in her bedroom. I had done a pan of the empty room, making sure to include Delaney's sleeping form resting on my lap.

Her phone started ringing, but it wasn't until the second call that she sprang up from my lap, trying to wake up. "What..."

"Your phone's ringing," I said helpfully.

She stretched her arm across the bed to grab it from the center of the bed, blinking, still trying to awaken. "Holy crap," she breathed as she looked at her phone. "How long have I been asleep?"

"Not long," I assured her.

The phone rang in her hand again and, this time, she answered it. "Ava?" Delaney sat up straighter as she said, "Whoa, wait..." Her eyes flew to mine, and she lowered her phone below her chin. Eyes narrowed, she said, "What did you do?" I shrugged a shoulder, but before she could rip me a new one, Ava called her attention back to the phone. "No...I just woke up. I...no...you're kidding me, Ava...*What!?*" Delaney shot me an incredulous look before saying, "Let me call you back, okay? Yeah. No. Yeah, I'll pull it up now. Yeah, let me call you back."

I stayed seated watching Delaney shaking her head at me. "Tell me she's lying, Deke," she implored. "Please, please, please tell me Ava wasn't...that this is a joke..."

"I can't," I stated simply. "Pull it up, Delaney."

Her hands were trembling as her fingers flew across the screen until she came upon my social media real-time video. I didn't say anything, but you could hear my voice loud and clear in the quiet stillness of the room. Because, here's the thing...I humiliated Delaney in public, and so, she deserved an apology in public, and this was the only way I could think of to do it.

The video begins by panning Delaney's room, showcasing the emptiness of it, and then her sleeping on my lap on her bed, and finally me. "So, by now, most everyone probably knows about the showdown at the cove Saturday night. You've all probably heard about how I was hanging out with my friends, while a girl I was seeing walked upon us, and I kept on with my business. You probably heard about how I ripped her to shreds by sharing her utmost secrets. You probably heard how Deke Marlow used up Delaney Martin and tossed her aside." In the video, I'm shaking my head. "But that's not, *at all*, what happened...

What happened was that I saw a picture of my girlfriend with someone else, and instead of letting her explain, I let my insecurities get the best of me, because, trust me when I tell you this girl makes me feel insecure like a motherfucker. See, she's better than me. She's better than me in every way. So, when I assumed the worst, I let a girl who means nothing to me sit on my lap to make Delaney jealous. I did it to hide just how torn in half I was by her supposed betrayal. But because Delaney is stronger than I had given her credit for, she walked away with her dignity still intact. So, because I was too weak to face that she might not love me, I chased after her and spewed the most vicious things about her, all of which were untrue. Nothing I said that night was true. It was all hateful shit spewed by a guy who couldn't handle losing the best thing that's ever happened to him...

When I found out the truth, I chased her down, begged for forgiveness, and gave her no choice but to forgive me or suffer for it. I ignored her protests and ignored how she told me she didn't love me anymore. More importantly, I ignored how I don't deserve her and refused to back down...

Delaney Martin is the fucking air I breathe; I can't afford to back down...

She hasn't forgiven me, and she probably never will...and, well, I don't blame her if she doesn't, because what I did to her was not love. It was selfish insecurity, and she has every right to walk away from me. As you can see from the beginning of this video, her room is empty because she's moving. She was secretly moving away so I couldn't find her...

But I won't let her...

I love Delaney, and I will spend every day of the rest of my life living on my knees for her. I will live for her, kill for her, and die for her if she asks...

Delaney, baby...I'm so fucking sorry. I'm sorrier than you will ever know, but I'll never let you go...

Ever."

Delaney was sobbing by the time the video cut off. Her phone in her lap, her face was in her hands, sobbing, and it was the most heartbreaking thing I have ever witnessed. She was crying as if her soul was being torn to pieces.

I crawled to her on the bed and gathered her up in my arms, letting her cry it all out. "I'm sorry, baby," I whispered over, and over into her hair. "I'm so goddamn sorry, Lamb."

My heart started beating again, and my relief was palpable when Delaney turned in my arms and tried to bury herself inside my chest. She was crawling and moving like she couldn't get close enough to me, and the more she burrowed herself to me, the tighter I held onto her.

When she finally looked up at me, she sobbed out the most painful and beautiful words I will ever hear in my life, "I love you, Deke."

"Thank Christ," I swore right before she tucked her face into my neck and continued to cry.

It was hours later when she finally woke up again from crying herself to sleep, and my body was feeling it. I hadn't moved a muscle because I had refused to let her go, even in her sleep.

"Deke?" she mumbled sleepily.

"I'm here, baby," I muttered into her hair.

She was quiet for a bit before saying, "I bought a house in Manotile, and-"

"We'll sell it this week after moving you into my place," I said, interrupting her. No fucking way was she going to live in Manotile.

I thought she might argue because, let's face it, that video wasn't shit enough to going towards earning her forgiveness, but she didn't. Instead, she said, "You can never hurt me again like that, Deke. I'll walk and never look back."

I bit the inside of my cheek enough to taste blood, and I knew I was going to have to talk to Ramsey some more about how he deals with what he did to Emerson.

I positioned Delaney so she was straddling my lap and she had to look at me. Her face was a puffy mess, but she still looked breathtaking. "Delaney, I meant what I said in that video," I replied. "I am going to spend the rest of my life making sure you never doubt what you mean to me."

"Forgiving you makes me feel stupid," she admitted, and I understood. No one wanted to be the fool who forgave someone, only to be proven wrong later on.

"I get that, Lamb," I whispered. "I do. I understand your pride is taking a beating, I do. But, Delaney, I will do whatever you need me to do to make that feeling go away. If you need me to beg you during lunch in front of everyone at school, I'll do it. If you need all my money, my car, whatever…it's *yours*. If you need me to never even look at another girl again for the rest of my life, I'll do it."

The tears came back, but they were quiet and tender, not violent and heartbreaking. "I don't know what I need," she confessed. "I don't know how to make this feeling go away."

I brushed her hair back from her face. "Maybe talking with Emerson might help," I suggested.

Her eyes lit up a little as she agreed, "Maybe." Delaney's eyes searched mine before saying, "I need you to need me above everything and everyone else, Deke."

I smirked. "I already do, Delaney."

She fell against me, and I held her some more as I let her come to terms with her new future. I knew it was going to be a hard fight until Delaney believed what I was telling her, but I was up for it. Delaney Martin was everything I never knew would consume me.

I spent a lot of time teasing Ramsey and Liam about how they worshipped the girls but having Delaney in my life made me see that love truly is a maddening sickness.

Here's the only person in the entire world who holds your heart, mind, and soul in the palm of their hands, and the idea that something could happen to them, or they could leave you?

Yeah, Delaney wasn't ever leaving my sight again.

EPILOGUE

Deke – Ten Years Later ~

Vacation has finally started, and I couldn't wait.

It's been about two years since I've taken an actual vacation, and it was showing if Ramsey and Liam telling me to go suck a dick this morning was any indication.

Ten years, and a shit ton of hard work later, we were equal partners in our own company, and life couldn't be more perfect.

Actually, that's a lie. It got infinitely a lot better as I snuck up on Delaney in the kitchen and wrapped my arms around her.

"Deke!" she screeched.

"Expecting someone else?" I teased.

Delaney turned around in my arms and smirked up at me. "You scared the crap out of me," she grumbled.

I looked down at my lovely wife and asked, "Where are your hellacious offspring?"

She laughed and just shook her head and then narrowed her eyes at me. "Emerson came and got them. Roselyn and Liam are having some sort of Deke's-Gone-Let-Celebrate party or something and everyone's at their place."

I laughed. "Uh, the guys might have mentioned this morning they'll be happy to be free of me for two weeks when I accused Lee of hiding my coffee creamer…uh, that was sitting on the kitchenette in broad daylight for the entire world to see."

She smiled. "An innocent mistake," she said, defending me like the loyal wife she was.

"Uh…we were throwing punches at the time of this 'innocent' mistake," I mumbled.

Delaney laughed and said, "No wonder Emerson came and got the kids. She was probably afraid you'd snap at one of them, and then I'd have to kill you."

"Speaking of kids," I lowered onto my haunches, "how's this little girl doing?" Delaney was pregnant with our fourth child, and she just started showing a couple of weeks ago.

We had three boys and were finally getting a girl. And, while Delaney didn't know this, I had planned on continuing to knock her up until she did give me a girl. Dash was eight, Crew was six, and Zane was four, and as much as I loved my sons, I really wanted a little girl.

Ten years ago, after I moved Delaney in with me, Ramsey, Liam, and I had told our parents to go eat a dick and we started up our own company. The girls had gone to college, but they had all gone to Blaineview, where they got an exceptional education, and received their degrees. The only reason we had managed to survive them going to school while we worked to get our company off the ground was because we knew they were all together.

They'd protect each other.

And when Dash came into the world, Ramsey and Emerson had produced the first of their two boys, Ramsey Jr. and Maddox. Liam and Roselyn fell in line with their three children, Chance, Neo, and Gideon. The entire brood was made up of boys, except for Ava's kids. She was able to throw some estrogen in the mix with her two girls, DJ (Delaney Jr.) and sweet little Maggie.

And, now, Delaney was finally giving me a little girl.

"Other than zapping all my energy, she's doing well," Delaney complained lovingly.

I leaned down and nuzzled her neck. "How zapped are we talking about?"

Delaney's laugh turned into a moan when I reached around and took her ass in both my hands. "I'm not *that* zapped," she answered huskily.

Grabbing Delaney by the back of her thighs, I hoisted her up and planted her fine ass on the kitchen counter. Stepping in between her legs, I took her face in my hands and kiss her, pouring everything I felt for her in that kiss.

Ramsey had been right all those years ago.

The regret I felt at how I treated Delaney all those years ago at the cove has stayed with me every day since then. I did my best to treasure her daily, and I knew she was happy with our lives-happy with me, but it wasn't enough for me. It's been ten years, but I will spend the rest of my days loving Delaney like I should have from the beginning.

I broke off the kiss to tell her, "I love you, Lamb."

She smiled softly because she recognized my tone. "I know you do, Deke. I love you, too."

The End.

PLAYLIST

Series Playlist – The Right Kind Of Wrong – LeAnn Rimes

Facing the Enemy – Pretty Girl – Sugarcult
Aerials – Systems Of A Down
Animals – Maroon 5
Centuries – Fall Out Boy
The Catalyst – Linkin Park
Hail Mary – 2Pac
Killing Strangers – Marilyn Manson
Sucker For Pain – Lil' Wayne
Whatever It Takes – Imagine Dragons
Engaging the Enemy – Basic Instinct – The Acid
Addicted – Saving Abel
Dollhouse – Melanie Martinez
If You Could Only See – Tonic
Like A Stone – Audioslave
Unforgettable – French Montana
Where You Belong – The Weeknd
Piano In The Dark – Brenda Russell
I Shall Believe – Sheryl Crow
Battling the Enemy – She – Live
Love The Way You Lie – Eminem
Broken – Seether
I Wanna Be Bad – Willa Ford
Pray For Me – The Weeknd
I Knew You Were Trouble – Taylor Swift
Irresistible (Remix) – Jessica Simpson
Pray – JRY
Starboy – The Weeknd
Provoking the Enemy – Lighthouse – Live
Dark Horse – Katy Perry
Say It Right – Nelly Furtado
I'm Bad At Love – Maddy Benson
By The Way – Hinder
Run Away – Live
All Or Nothing – Theory Of A Deadman
Savin' Me – Nickelback
Wolves – Selena Gomez

ABOUT THE AUTHOR

M.E. Clayton works full-time and writes as a hobby. She is an avid reader and, with much self-doubt, but more positive feedback and encouragement from her friends and family, she took a chance at writing, and the Seven Deadly Sins Series was born. Writing is a hobby she is now very passionate about. When she's not working, writing, or reading, she is spending time with her family or friends. If you care to learn more, you can read about her by visiting the following:

Smashwords Interview at:
 https://www.smashwords.com/interview/MonClayton
Bookbub Author Page at:
 https://www.bookbub.com/profile/m-e-clayton
Goodreads Author Page:
 https://www.goodreads.com/MEClayton

CONTACT ME

I really appreciate you reading my book and I would love to hear from you! Now, unfortunately, because I do have a full-time job, and a family I love spending time with, at this time, I'm afraid it would be very hard for me to maintain a multitude of social media sites. However, for the sites I do participate in, here are my social media coordinates:

Favorite my Smashwords Author Page:
 https://www.smashwords.com/interview/MonClayton
Like my Facebook Author Page:
 https://facebook.com/claytonbooks
Follow my Bookbub Author Page:
 https://www.bookbub.com/profile/m-e-clayton
Follow my Goodreads Author Page:
 https://www.goodreads.com/MEClayton
Visit my Website at:
 https://meclayton2016.wixsite.com/mysite

OTHER BOOKS

Please visit your favorite book retailer to discover other books by
M.E. Clayton:

The Seven Deadly Sins Series (In Order)
Catching Avery (Avery & Nicholas)
Chasing Quinn (Quinn & Chase)
Claiming Isabella (Isabella & Julian)
Conquering Kam (Kamala & Kane)
Capturing Happiness

The Buchanan Brothers Series (In Order)
If You Could Only See (Mason & Shane)
If You Could Only Imagine (Aiden & Denise)
If You Could Only Feel (Gabriel & Justice)
If You Could Only Believe (Michael & Sophia)
If You Could Only Dream

The How To: Modern Day Woman's Guide Series (In Order)
How to Stay Out of Prison; A Modern Day Woman's Guide (Lyrical & Nixon)
How to Keep Your Job; A Modern Day Woman's Guide (Alice & Lincoln)
How to Maintain Your Sanity; A Modern Day Woman's Guide (Rena & Jackson)

The Enemy Series (In Order)
Facing the Enemy (Deke & Delaney)
Engaging the Enemy (Roselyn & Liam)
Battling the Enemy (Deke & Delaney)
Provoking the Enemy (Ava & Ace)
Loving the Enemy

The Enemy Duet (In Order)
In Enemy Territory (Fiona & Damien)
On Enemy Ground (Victoria & William)

Standalone
Unintentional
Purgatory, Inc.
My Big, Huge Mistake
An Unexpected Life
The Heavier The Chains....

52962444R00102

Made in the USA
Lexington, KY
26 September 2019